GOD AWFUL

REBEL

S. ACEVEDO

THREE
POINTS
PUBLISHING

The text type was set in Adobe Caslon

ISBN 978-0-9863207-8-1 (hardcover)
ISBN 978-0-9863207-9-8 (eBook)
Library of Congress Control Number: 2019930749

First Edition
Printed in the United States of America
15 16 17 18 19 — 6 5 4 3 2 1

For my children,
Corina, Antonia, and Armando,
who inspire, encourage, and beguile.

CONTENTS

1. INTENTION 1

2. THE DARK 12

3. INTRODUCING THE NEEBO 15

4. MOUNTS 25

5. VISION 31

6. COUNCIL COLOSSUS 33

7. COUNCIL CHAMBERS 39

8. IMPACT 53

9. AVERSION 62

10. SIEGE 69

11. ADVANTAGE 75

12. A SLIPPERY TAIL 83

13. THE MAGGOTS MOVE 89

14. CRUSH 92

15. OVERRUN 98

16. ENTRY 109

17. GOAT 121

18. REWARD 131

19. NATURE 138

20. THE SNAKES STRIKE 146

21. UNRAVELED 160

22. BLOOD FROM A STONE 170

23. PAST MADE PRESENT 174

24. CHARMING THE SNAKES 181

25. FIGHTING NO BODY 196

26. HELP 204

27. PERCEPTION 212

28. DO'S 226

29. DON'T'S 238

WHO'S WHO IN ORDER OF REFERENCE 250

Q&A WITH THE AUTHOR 258

ACKNOWLEDGMENTS 274

ABOUT THE AUTHOR 275

Chapter 1

INTENTION

I was unconvinced that the god of love might actually *be* in love. Cupid never seemed to really understand it, so naturally I doubted that any happenstance of deep, romantic love might stick. Still, even cynics like me want to believe.

I am celibate. Gloriously so. And, as goddess of the hunt, I don't tolerate meddling males who would try to capture my free spirit and suppress my athleticism to impose their values upon me – much less claim me as their own. That's my experience with the sentiment of love. Still, I won't begrudge others their choices.

"One hundred rings, Diana," Cupid said, "for the first hundred years Tamara and I spend together." He handed me a one-of-a-kind arrow. Its tip was a single, giant blue diamond. Its fletching was made of long white feathers tinged with blue. I recognized them as Cupid's own flight feathers. The arrow's shaft was wrapped in luxurious blue velvet and encircled by those hundred rings, each unique and enchanting.

My heart pinged. How odd. Sentimentality normally has no home in my heart. I suspected that Cupid was the culprit. I shielded my body and mind from the persuasive mojo that he was likely carelessly throwing around.

He couldn't be doing it on purpose. He'd better not be. I decided to remind him just who he was dealing with.

Rather than turn Cupid into a toad or a worm, I whistled my stag to my side. The magnificent buck is my near constant companion. He's strong and agile, yet sensitive and yielding – all that a male creature should be. We have an understanding. We respect each other's power and autonomy, and he reminds everyone that those who attempt to sway me with their charms will end badly.

I felt tension positively roll off Cupid. Oh, yes, my stag did indeed remind him of Actaeon, that overeager male who centuries ago stumbled into my woods and lingered to spy. The mortal slunk his way close enough to catch me bathing, and his perverse curiosity cost him dearly. I spotted him. He tried to run, but he'd have been better off begging for mercy. As punishment for both his crime and attempted escape, I transformed him into a stag. He became clumsy as a newborn fawn, and his eyes ran red when I set his own hunting hounds against him. Their snarls were almost as loud as his screams when they tore him to shreds.

I've relaxed a bit since then.

Cupid may have been counting on that when he beckoned me.

"Great Huntress, Great Huntress, a captive begs your time," he'd called. The "begging" part is what pleased me, and I found him burning incense at a holly grove, fanning the curls of smoke upward with his wings. He immediately apologized for the interruption. "I know we don't see each other often, Diana. My work keeps me near people and away from woodlands."

Little did he know that I did not take his regular absence as disrespect. If I wanted visitors, I wouldn't live tucked away in the woods.

After hearing his elaborate plan, which made a show of his intentions, well, I couldn't arbitrarily stand in his way. He might even finally be sincere, I reasoned, having only taken millennia to get there.

I turned the elegant arrow over in my fingers and gazed at the rings. I was impressed by their extravagance and the trouble Cupid must have gone through. Here was a vibrant jade stone, green as new grass, set atop a silver band engraved with winding French poetry. Another ring presented a rosy opal perched atop a circle of interweaving golden threads, reminding me of the braids of my nymphs. Such joyful creatures. And this ring, my favorite, was a simple wooden ring, its dark and light bands of grain breathtaking beneath a clear glaze.

"I flew the heavens and Earth to find the best artisans," Cupid said. "I'd give Tamara a new ring every day if she'd let me."

Cupid babbled a bit about how he secured others' help. Either he was trying to make polite conversation or trying to convince me to be a part of his scheme. I gave him as bored a look as I could muster. My patience runs thin at affectation. Cupid got the hint and stopped talking. When I nodded, he gave a quick thanks and flew off.

Two mornings later, I was alerted through the eyes of my harrier hawk that the moment was here. I mounted my stag and flattened my hands atop his coat for godly speed. We stotted fast as the wind to a tree-lined mesa near the supposedly happy couple. It was a beautiful spot, encircled by trees yet open to the cliff and a breathtaking view of the sea beyond. I could smell tangy earth, sharp sea spray, and ambrosia-fed Celestials in a single whiff. I looked around and saw branches moving. The woods were filling with hidden co-conspirators. We moved to the woods as well and settled within the shadows. I slid off my stag's back and fit a ring onto each of his antler tines. He made for a magnificent sight: twitching, muscled power below elegant artistry.

I watched again through my hawk's eyes as Cupid and Tamara bounded up the seaside cliffs, heading our way. They wore brown leather tunics. His was longer and darker looking against his white skin, hers shorter and lighter against her brown skin. I noticed Cupid used a leather guard on his left arm and finger tabs on his right. Tamara apparently needed different protection from the arrow's chafing, seeing that she used two gloves. They ascended, firing arrows at hay bales wrapped in paper targets. The bales made poor substitutes for humans bustling along an urban street unaware of impending love, but I suppose practice is practice.

Tamara risked leaning off some wedged rocks to hit the most inaccessible targets. Well, what woman or goddess wouldn't want to prove herself when competing against one of the best archers on heaven and earth? I say *one* of the best because I have yet to be beaten – unlike my twin brother, Apollo. A story for another time.

My hawk's vision zoomed in on Cupid's face in time to see him stop and smile at Tamara as if she were a brook in paradise. I think I rolled my eyes high enough to see my brain – and then felt immediate shame. Skeptic though I was, I should not mock the very union I'd agreed to bless.

Cupid continued making his way up the cliff, stealthily leading Tamara to the plateau. He took Tamara's gloved hand and walked her to the center while hundreds of hidden Celestials watched. Cupid swept his free arm overhead. The clouds above them gathered thick and wavy, like buttercream frosting.

That was my brother's cue. Rays of sunlight piled up against the clouds.

Cupid waved his hand again, and the center section of clouds dissipated. It left a heart-shaped hole, as if Cupid had pulled a massive cookie cutter from the frosting. When warm sunlight cascaded through the opening, it cast a love-shaped spotlight upon them.

Tamara looked at the ground around her and laughed, to her hidden audience's delight.

Cupid pointed upward, and Apollo drifted through the breach. My twin wore his usual sleeveless, white tunic, gathered at the waist with twisted, golden thread. The darn-near dress ended just above his knees and fluttered dangerously higher as he floated downward. Knowing him, he was naked underneath and didn't mind if anyone found out. Those who had seen him – his face, I mean – described him as handsome, which I suppose made me the same. He had dark brown hair and eyes and golden skin. Well, tugging the sun across the sky all day has to give you a year-round tan. He also had a ready smile – *too* ready for anyone who happened to catch his interest down on Earth. The playboy. Apollo was stroking his lyre, which he rarely does on demand. Cupid must have asked verrrrrrrry nicely – or promised to owe him one. Risky.

Tamara stepped back from the descending god of light and crossed her ankles to curtsy, but Cupid drew her arm upward to bring her back to full height.

Apollo landed some ten meters before her and toned down his bright aura. He always waited until the last possible moment to do that, so that the brightness would awe his audience.

His dimming was my cue.

My stag lowered himself for me to mount once more, and together we entered the clearing. He promenaded slowly, regally. The rings on his antlers glinted at every movement. I caught Apollo flicking his fingers, like a child playing with marbles, pinging the rings with superfine sunbeams to make them dazzle.

I stared into Tamara's eyes and witnessed fear cross them. She recognized me, and she'd bow unless Cupid stopped her, as is fitting. A god's chosen mate becomes royalty herself. Tamara stutter-stepped when Cupid grabbed her arm.

Her mouth suddenly formed an O, and I think she caught on: the heart in the sky, the sparkling rings, and a couple of gods – plus many minor Celestials she still hadn't seen – don't just show up at a playful competition without reason.

My stag stopped before her and rolled his head to each side.

Cupid's cue. He dropped to one knee.

Tamara put a hand over her mouth. It was a curious reaction, but one that I'd seen before, as if women feared that talking might make a suitor change his mind. I suppose it could. In such a circumstance, *I* might make the same gesture – to hold back vomit. My life allowed me no other reaction.

"Tamara, my darling, ma chérie," Cupid began. "For eons I've sparked desperate and lasting love in the hearts of countless beings. I thought I knew love's power and intricacies better than anyone ever in the history of time. But I didn't. *You* taught me love, my treasure. Only you can turn my every moment into joy. Only you can make my – and every – heart sing.

"Tamara, I love only you. Let me show my undying love over the vast expanse of ages. Will you marry me? Will you be mine and me yours to share all eternity?" He covered his heart with both hands.

That gesture was my stag's cue. He bent his head and presented the hundred curious and creative rings. Tamara's eyes widened to the size of tea saucers. Cupid, still kneeling, reached for a ring, removed it, and petted my stag in thanks. This was off-script and potentially dangerous. My stag scarcely allows *my* hand upon him. Strange then that my stag twitched just once before calming. Perhaps Cupid's ultra-loving sentiments extended to his reach. Or maybe my stag sensed Cupid's desire to impress his animal-loving girlfriend. Word had spread even so far as to my woods that Tamara had tamed Pluto's three-headed hellhound and managed to enchant Bacchus' panthers. Bet the god of wine felt a buzzkill after that.

Cupid lifted his hand off my stag, smiled at Tamara, and raised the ring to her.

That was undeniably her cue.

Would she put her hand in his and allow him to slip the first of many rings upon her finger? Could she look past his centuries of arrogant womanizing and foolhardy self-aggrandizement?

Spoiler alert, I wouldn't. The rings looked like nothing more than pretty manacles to me.

But love makes people foolish, from what I've heard. It certainly had that effect on all the other Celestials and mortals I'd seen over the millennia. Lust has the same effect, but no one could witness this grand declaration and confuse it with lust.

Tamara's eyes softened and shone with reflected rapture. The hand that had covered her mouth had fallen at some point to her heart, as if she hoped to quiet its beating, lest it be heard by the outside world. I found it both cliché and adorable. *She,* at least, loved *him,* even though males are so tragically *male.* I looked to my brother's eyes and saw no guilt or contemplation despite his being as big a womanizer as Cupid had been – and Jupiter and Neptune still are – and even Pluto, who outright stole his woman.

Movement drew my eyes back to Tamara. She planted both hands on either side of Cupid's pudgy, ruddy face and ran a thumb along one bushy eyebrow. Cupid's brown curly hair waved in the breeze like seaweed in the current. Tamara's black, wavy hair brushed across her shoulders at each gust. She bent to kiss him – respectfully, considering her public audience.

"Yes," she breathed aloud after drawing away. "Yes, I'll marry you."

Several hundred of the angels that Cupid and Tamara restored to Olympus set to flight. Tamara started at the rush of wings and stir of branches. Cupid leapt to his feet. The Celestials filled the sky and burst into song, a literal heavenly chorus. Apollo shone rays of pink and golden light everywhere, shooting them off his fingers like the outlaw of a Wild West showdown.

"Oh my gods," Tamara said in a breath. "I can't believe this. And look!" She pointed at three angels flying out of the crowd and toward them, all wearing white suits: a rotund, pink-faced redhead; a brown-skinned smiler with a thin mustache; and a much darker-skinned, dapper angel who carried himself with authority. Behind them was a buggy creature, ostensibly a cherub, flapping his transparent wings if he were in a raging wind tunnel. I noticed he wore a winged hat and sandals, and I immediately remembered they'd belonged to Mercury before the god of thieves was banished.

The angels dropped hard in front of Tamara and enveloped her in rough arms. The cherub followed seconds later.

"Cornelius! Tommy! Tyrone!" Tamara shouted in surprise and gasping for breath. "And Pip! Oh, how wonderful you're here! And Jarel?"

"Still trainin' with this one's dad," Tommy answered, pointing at Cupid, then turning to face him. "Glad ta see yer finally making this hookup honest, Junior."

Cupid narrowed his eyes ever so slightly. I wondered if I'd witnessed an insult – always dangerous when levied against a god – but Cupid grinned, laughed, and pulled the troublemaker in for a half-hug-half-handshake sort of thing. I decided the Fabulous Fallen Four must be as close as the rumors say – minus the one playing war intern.

"Jarel do say hi," Tommy said to Tamara.

I stood corrected.

As they pattered on, I turned toward the woods and raised my hand. The thousand birds I'd summoned burst into flight and formed a wide and colorful halo encircling everyone overhead. They twittered with joy.

Scores of rainbows shot across the waters just beyond the cliffs, and I realized Neptune must have been brought into the plans as well. I imagined Cupid thanking the constellations for friends in high places.

Cupid snagged Tamara's waist and twirled her with unbridled happiness.

I swallowed a lump and realized that this truly was a moment I was glad to have witnessed. There's a lot to be cynical about, especially over the course of an eternal life. But not this. This was true love – and a glorious proposal.

I'd give them a full day together before breaking the news.

Chapter 2

THE DARK

The next morning as I sprinted through the forest, racing my stags as usual to keep us fit and ready for action, a vision broke through my consciousness. I skidded to a halt and grabbed a tree for support. The stags charged on, perhaps sensing a ruse. This wasn't one. This was the strongest vision of the past three days. It felt urgent, as if its messenger knew its significance. Bats normally ignore the goings-on of people, but this one knew that someone sneaking around her particular cave was cause for great alarm.

I let the vision overtake me. I was underground. In the distance and overhead, bulky, uneven shapes hung from the rough ceiling. Clicks and chirps from my host took the place of sound, and the faraway shapes pulsed as if they were pictures on a vibrating drum. Everything was black on black, yet I could sense direction – and movement. Something was definitely moving. The bat's echolocation was a primitive vision, monotone and relative. A few more clicks and I saw the ceiling shift as if an ocean waved overhead.

I channeled my command, and the bat strummed sound in every direction, giving me a clearer view of his dark and dreary home. We were in the largest cavern I'd seen in my long existence. It was massive, many times larger than even Vulcan's lair, although the god of volcanoes has so many tunnels and secret passageways that one can only guess at his home's true expanse.

The ceiling here moved in a way I hadn't expected, and, ho, I spotted hundreds of small insects scurrying about it. Ah, I realized. The ceiling was the ground. My bat was hanging upside-down. I imagined the many kinds of bugs that would thrive in the guano and cool dampness of cave life.

But wait. Another click shook the image, and the moving shape reappeared up high, shuffling away from my host into the cavern's vast, open space.

"Fly," I commanded. "Find a perch to stand upright."

A battery of clicks and the whole scene moved and spun as we flew out of our crevice into the main expanse. My bat banked sharply and turned back toward a small ledge. She alit there and settled her wings like forefeet. I sensed her discomfort, her clumsiness, but I demanded she be still.

With the image righted, I could better understand what was happening. A hunched figure limped away from my scout, turning its head side to side and occasionally stooping as if hoping to avoid detection. It was slowly and carefully making its way in. My host raised her head and clicked.

I gasped. Taking up the entirety of the cavern's

far side – and my host's distant vision – was a giant shape pacing within a cage. It reached its hand toward the many thin, vibrating rails of the cage. When its hand connected, sparks flew. The mass recoiled and flailed in seeming rage.

My scout's echolocation wasn't letting me see anything with clarity. "Look toward the ground," I ordered. My bat did so, and, in an instant, I transferred my connection into the mind of a cockroach at the hulk's feet.

"Rise," I commanded. "Up, up."

I heard the insect's exoskeleton snap as it rose and bent its back in a way not naturally intended. I held it still as I saw through its eyes. More monochromatic black on black. More vague shapes. I couldn't mistake the meaning of the small, slinking shape reaching the huddled colossus and breaking the bars that bound it.

I felt antennae and legs all around me. Scurrying. Uncountable clicks. I transported back into my bat's mind just as she and a million others burst into flight in abject terror. Screeches. Collisions. Bouncing off walls and one another.

I forced my bat to look back. The shape had grown legs and was thundering toward her, toward escape. It was gaining. It overtook my bat's vision.

She shrieked.

And in an instant, I was back in my woods.

The bat, I knew, was dead.

Chapter 3

INTRODUCING THE NEEBO

Time passes differently for the gods. When eternity lies ahead of you, a day zips by faster than the flight of a hummingbird. After the cave vision and during the day of peace I'd promised Cupid, I channeled my divination skills to catch snippets of his whereabouts.

First he took Tamara to a deserted island to frolic in the frothing surf and to picnic on the velvety white beach. They were a postcard couple in white capris and breezy tops. Then they walked off their meal, meandering the hills and winding roads of a small Greek town. Finally they settled for the evening beside a waterfall deep within the Amazon Rainforest, in a clearing untrod by the foot of man.

Air travel is impossible for my stags, so I called for my international transportation, which delivered me to a spot just above the jungle canopy about a quarter mile away from the seclusion-seeking lovebirds. I thanked my reclusive friends, knowing they'd be introduced to Cupid and Tamara soon enough, and I dismissed them to find nearby shelter. I then leapt into the canopy.

The branches were supple and bent sharply under my weight. As the goddess of untamed woods, I felt powerful here and very much at home. I grabbed some sprigs to slow my fall, wrecking them in the process, dropped through giant leaves and tangled vines, and landed softly on the spongy jungle ground below. I clicked my tongue for local transportation. I heard a rustle to my left and watched a puma's head separate the fat red leaves of a low bush.

The puma stared at me, its golden eyes made more vibrant by the black lines framing them. Most pumas span seven feet from nose to tip of tail, but I could sense this one was much bigger. It probably stayed well in the shade to avoid humans and Celestials alike, even though it was armed with a jaw that could crush a skull and with claws that could spill the intestines of any of them. But of course this kitty wouldn't harm a fellow jungle friend. I approached and placed my hand on his sandy-brown cheek. He closed his eyes. We held the moment in peace until it was time to go. Then I patted him to return him to the moment and sat on his back for what I hoped would be a noisy approach.

I found Cupid and Tamara hand in hand in the clearing, smiling at each other, lovestruck. They were oblivious to my advancing swish of leaves, and I could see why. They were aglow in silver moonlight, bathed in the scent of wild flowers, and silhouetted by the shrouding spray of the waterfall on the far side of the clearing. I watched Cupid extend an arm toward the waterfall and wiggle his fingers to condense a mass of mist within the cascade. He swept the swell back to cocoon himself and his fiancée in a fragile privacy tent.

"Cuuuuupid," I called in warning. "Tamara."

The lovers leapt to their feet within the tent, splashing a hole right through its top. They sputtered. I did feel sorry for them.

"H-hello," Tamara stammered. She nudged Cupid, who gave an uneasy wave.

I nodded at the pair and said, "You're wanted at Council."

"W-wha?" Cupid asked. "Now? I'm wanted *now?* By who?"

I stared at Cupid and saw his face scrunch with an educated guess.

"Ugh! Why can't he ever just *talk* to me?!"

I was stopped from answering by new visions popping in my head, relays from faraway animals frozen in fear. I felt their terror, their muscles tense, their eyes widen, but I knew that to help their kind meant I had to focus on the moment. I looked to the privacy tent, which remained perfectly intact except where Cupid and Tamara had burst the top. They'd look even more absurd if they didn't diffuse that tent soon, and we had some urgency to do so. Far behind them, the narrow, three-story virgin waterfall continued its breathtaking torrent.

"Honey, Jupiter's a busy god," Tamara answered in my stead.

"He's also my *grandfather*. Why doesn't he at least send parchment like everyone else in the administration?"

I knew Cupid referred to those notes written on scraps of parchment that pop into existence next to their intended recipient and disappear with their reply. I rarely need them as I am biologically tuned in to anyone who might ever send or receive one – and that would include Cupid and Tamara in just a few minutes.

"Why does Jupiter want to see me *now?*" Cupid asked.

I turned my gaze to Tamara who I knew would exhibit more insight than her off-put lover.

"Cupid, we're being disrespectful to the goddess before us. Forgive us, please," she said, curtsying her courtesy before Cupid could stop her. I looked away. She'd have to learn to break that particular habit. It would soon be a social misstep, rising in rank as she is. Even the constant curtsying and bowing of lesser Celestials ruffles me enough to avoid Olympus.

"Sorry," Cupid said, either for his own rudeness or for failing to stop his fiancée's faux pas. "Thank you for delivering the message, Diana. But, wait. Why would you be delivering a message? Why didn't Jupiter send Pip?"

I was pleased that he recognized the breach in protocol and came to the thrust of things. I haven't physically delivered more than a handful of messages in all eternity.

"I do not deliver the message of another."

Cupid and Tamara exchanged surprised looks.

"Oh my," Tamara murmured.

"Oh no," Cupid replied. "You're telling me directly that I'm wanted at Council ... because you're the one who wants me there?"

"Jupiter expects you to succeed him – or at least take command in his occasional absence," I said.

"But you want me there now," Cupid said.

I stared on.

"You should go," Tamara said, even as Cupid put his face in his hands and muttered something about seers and the trouble they bring. Tamara swept her hand through the water pup tent, which broke apart and rose as mist.

"I am a god," Cupid answered, ignoring her tidying. "Within the past year, I – with help – saved the kingdom not once but twice. Why am I constantly summoned from my leisure?"

"Because," I answered with an impatient finality, "you are so often at leisure. Great power has been placed upon your shoulders. The greater the power, the heavier the chains that bind you."

Cupid sent Tamara a positively withered look. I think even his curly mop of hair sagged in resignation.

Of course, as a prescient goddess, a prophetess, I foresaw his eventual understanding because I did indeed see him at Council, but it was time to end the divination and worm my way directly into his thoughts.

"Do not dismay, Cupid," I said. "I bring a gift to lift spirits."

"But I wasn't unhappy until you got h-,"

Tamara elbowed him hard in the ribs. He winced and bent to soothe the strike. She cleared her expression as if hoping I hadn't noticed.

"I mean," Cupid corrected with a cough, "how kind."

I wondered – not for the first time – whether my intervention was wise, but a prophetess can only see possible futures, not which path prevails.

"Yes, Diana," Tamara added. She must have sensed my hesitation. "Thank you for your thoughtfulness. Your gift is altogether unexpected and very generous."

I could see why everyone thought so highly of her. Cupid would need her diplomacy. I swung my leather quiver from my back to my chest to access its exterior pocket. I unwound the flap's strap from the button securing it and withdrew a bouquet of flowers.

Cupid's brows scrunched together. He stared a moment too long, cleared his throat, and asked, "You, um, you brought me flowers?"

"Yes."

"Um, ha. I'm flattered, really," he said, "but are you trying to make Tamara jealous?"

Tamara's jaw dropped. "Cupid!"

"What?" he asked with a shrug. "The lady comes half way around the world to deliver me flowers and asks me to go with her."

"The goddess," Tamara corrected. "And the goddess of chastity, Cupid, who's slain men who've insulted her for less than you're doing right now. I mean ... oh ... I'm sorry, Diana."

She wasn't wrong even if it is dangerous to point out a goddess' flash points.

"Flowers," I said with deadpan severity, "always beguile." I held them at arm's length.

Cupid leaned forward to receive them and, once in hand, turned them over to skim a finger along the dried straw wrap gathering the bunch. "These are unusual flowers to choose for a bouquet. I guess I'm used to roses."

"And their message," I added.

Tamara shifted uncomfortably. "What are they, please?"

"The long purple flowers are monkshood. I've added blue Asian pigeonwings, pink snapdragons, and white poppies."

Tamara looked at me for more.

"It is wise to learn the ways of the wild," I said in answer to her unspoken question. I wondered if she would do so.

She leaned in to smell the bouquet. Cupid followed suit.

The moment they breathed in, I transported myself into the mind of one of the hundred neebo resting in the flowers' pollen, readying her and her tiny friends to enter their new hosts.

The neebo are transparent, winged creatures with legs as sensitive as tentacles. They pull their wonderfully slimy selves onto flower pollen or dust motes and act as a sort of contagion for me, allowing me unfettered access to those they inhabit. What they hear, I hear. What they see and feel, I do as well. The neebo are too small to be seen by mortals, yet they might be seen by the gods, were those gods inclined to perceive such little nippers. But noticing creatures which are easily overlooked requires a quiet presence that few employ.

The moment Cupid and Tamara inhaled, more deeply than I could have hoped, my friends the neebo were drawn in, pulled with pollen and scent to join the sentience of their new hosts. I returned to my own mind, but the neebo traveled up the lovers' noses and finally cozied themselves on their brains, in a space just for themselves. The transference, the possession really, was immediate, and Cupid's and Tamara's thoughts burst into my mind.

Mmmmm, these flowers smell wonderful, Tamara thought – and I heard.

Phew, the white ones have enough pollen to snuff out a horse. This was Cupid's lamentable thought, which I also heard.

I, as a prophetess who can see various futures, decided centuries ago that I needed to know what was going on in the gods' minds. So I fortuitously warned the neebo of impending human encroachment on their territory and then provided them sanctuary in my own woods. They feel forever indebted to me, and I am forever enriched. The neebo are my obliging little brain cooties.

Tamara's thoughts came in waves over a great many subjects; she needed fewer neebo so as to keep her brainwork from overwhelming me. Cupid's mind was far more silent than I'd expected, harboring fewer thoughts on a spattering of subjects; thus his every neebo was needed, save those who sought more fertile ground, as is their choice. I mentally nudged them to prompt sneezes. It adjusted the count.

"Gods bless you," I said.

The expelled neebo floated away to grab hold of a speck of whatever they'd come across. They always make do.

I raised my arms to call back my international transportation, which I assumed was sufficiently rested by now. Cupid and Tamara could fly and wouldn't need transport, but I did. Courtesy required that I provide for all.

"Our rides will be here shortly," I advised.

Tamara pulled off her sash belt and, with a flick, unraveled it into a wide, gauzy scarf, which she spread over the ground. She gathered their elegant picnic of ambrosia into a mound on the scarf. She then grabbed its far ends, lifted, and twirled. The result was a knapsack that resembled a cellophane-wrapped hard candy but with longer tufts. She draped one tuft over her shoulder and the other under the opposite arm and tied them together, instantly travel ready. Not a trace of their visit would remain other than their footprints. As it should be. Her actions pleased me.

A massive flapping sound above drew our eyes upward through the trees, where a winged creature overtook the bulk of the dusky sky: the quickest of my many griffins.

Chapter 4

MOUNTS

Oh gods! Cupid wailed in his thoughts.

Jupiter's crown, it's fantastic, Tamara whispered in her head.

I liked her reaction better.

My griffins are extraordinary. Their front halves are eagles. Their back ends are lions. These hybrids rose during Earth's infancy, when divisions were in chaos. Griffins survived the winnowing of species over the millennia and eventually became the stuff of myths. Those few mortals who caught glimpses of them and blathered at the local inn suffered great derision. I sometimes cannot process humans' disbelief. They so easily dismiss that outside their quotidian experiences.

The particularly fine griffin circling overhead was the fastest of my pride. His beak and facial feathers were light grey. He darkened to jet black at his wings. Only the tip of his tufted tail returned to grey, albeit speckled. He was made all the more beautiful by his intense eyes and imposing presence. He knew well his position as king of beasts.

He landed with a swoosh and bowed my way. I nodded in return and turned toward Tamara.

"No way," Cupid warned.

Yes way, Tamara thought, sporting an ear-to-ear grin trumpeting her excitement at a chance to ride a griffin. Few had ridden them, as the pride knows better than to flaunt itself.

"Whoa whoa whoa," interjected Cupid. "Who says we're okay with this? I'm not okay with this."

Tamara stepped to the griffin's side and waited in question. I nodded once more.

Thus assured of its obedience, Tamara held her palm under its razor-sharp beak. *Gorgeous,* I heard her think. The griffin snuffed and widened its stance a mere fraction.

"Now hold on just a minute!" Cupid protested, raising a hand.

I heard a half dozen thoughts pinging inside his skull, the usual overly protective, controlling twaddle. *Just who does Diana think she is?* And, *No one determines my travel but me.* Add, *Tamara can't just go off whichever way she wants.* To finally, *That thing looks dangerous!*

Point of fact, I *think* I'm a goddess. Beside that, I *know* I'm my own person who need not consult a guest for travel permissions. I looked to Tamara before I was tempted once more to turn Cupid into a toad or worm – or something worse.

Tamara seemed not at all inclined to take her eyes off an animal she'd just befriended, and so she moved her hand from under the griffin's beak to bury it within his feathery mane. She took hold and accepted his invitation by putting one foot on its bent leg and hopping aboard. She rested her knees in the crook of his wings.

"Hello," she said, releasing her grip to pet his shoulders with quick affection. "I'm Tamara. Thank you for the ride."

My griffin answered by shaking his feathered head. Tamara's laugh let slip that she found the sound of swooshing feathers quite satisfying.

"His name is Nightfall," I introduced on his behalf.

"Nightfall," she repeated and patted him once more.

In the few seconds this transpired, Cupid made no vocal demand that she seek *his* approval before accepting *mine*. Either this female had her male well trained in equal living or he dared not show disconfidence in my feathered friends. To his credit.

Another shadow fell across the clearing's waning light. We looked up to see my reddest griffin. She is the matriarch of the pride: strong, fierce, and quite ill tempered. There's almost no pleasing her. Cupid really had bad luck, and I felt not a whit sorry for him.

Dragon snot, Cupid thought.

The griffin landed with an aggressive thud in the center of the clearing, shaking her flaming red feathers and ending her whole-body quiver at the very tip of her deep brown tail. She raised her head lest anyone doubt her social standing.

I nodded my respects and glanced to Cupid. The griffin followed my gaze to assess her rider. Her hackles rose.

Not on your life, Cupid thought. "Um, you can take her, Diana. I don't mind flying."

Tamara turned her head toward him so quickly, she nearly toppled off Nightfall. I glared at Cupid.

The newly arrived griffin scratched deeply into the shallow, sandy soil of the Amazon jungle beneath her feet. She had been inconvenienced.

"We need fast transportation," I answered, "to make the meeting in time."

Another shadow overhead signified the arrival of my final griffin. Three griffins. He was expected to take one.

The god of love (toward *other* gods, I imagine, as thus far he was showing very little love toward me and my animals) sighed in his head and hurried to stand beside his griffin. I saw a multitude of bribes flash in his mind: offering a piece of ambrosia, shooting a bird dead to offer a meal, shooting *it* with a love arrow to ensure affection. He stopped on one thought and swirled his hands together. He opened them, revealing a water ball, which he held under the griffin's beak.

It was a peace gesture, water after a journey, but a risky one. I would not have been surprised had my pet chosen to sever Cupid's hand from his wrist as punishment.

Instead, she accepted the apology, to Cupid's visible relief. He looked back at me.

"Her name is Ember."

Oh gods, Cupid thought. He cleared his throat and recited the name aloud, "Ember." *As in, fire. Flames. Destruction.* He shook the thoughts away and tentatively placed a hand on Ember's shoulder. When she didn't attack, he climbed up, less gracefully than his fiancée and pulling a bit harder on a wing than he should have, but he hadn't had the easy help.

"I'm Cupid," he told Ember, "a god as surely as your mistress is a goddess, soooo…" He left the warning unfinished.

Ember stepped aside to allow the final landing before twilight. Down came a solid white griffin like a mythical ghost. This one was slightly older than his companions, the most recent pack leader before Nightfall. He landed softly and spread his expansive white wings, showing us he still had a great deal to be proud of. He flapped several times, fanning us with a cool breeze before folding them, his muscles rippling, thus displaying two of my preferred attributes: strength and discernment. One without the other is calamity.

I mounted and lay a hand upon his twitching shoulder. "Snowlight," I said for the benefit of my guests. "Griffins, to Council. Then return to your lair. Olympus will no longer be safe tonight. War begins."

"War?!" Cupid and Tamara asked together.

My griffins obeyed without hesitation. They tipped back onto their haunches, spread their enormous wings, and launched us into the crimson of a bloody sunset.

Chapter 5

VISION

We flew unusually high. The griffins took my warning seriously and were not about to risk our safety. Cupid bellowed questions about war and accusations of kidnapping while Tamara's silence belied her calm. *Diana is a seer*, she thought to herself. *What has she foreseen?*

Cupid nearly slipped off Ember and slung her a slew of disparaging thoughts. I noticed he didn't actually voice his insults. Ember might have tossed him for it. I pictured the scene prettily enough: Cupid tumbling for just a second or two before gaining his own flight, Ember charging him for not having the decency to die from descent, and a brutal sky battle between god and mythical beast. I enjoyed the imagery of such combat before my vision abruptly blurred. Nausea overtook me, and I plunged my hands into Snowlight's mane to grip every feather I could gather.

I trajected through the mind of one animal after another. I saw flashes of jungle plants. I felt leaves brush by. A scream rent the air. I leapt into the mind of another animal. Something pushed through the undergrowth. It was catching up. I heard howls. I landed in an animal looking at members of its own kind. White-headed capuchin – South American monkeys with blond faces. Their wide eyes were terrified. A dozen screams. They froze in fear and toppled off their branches. The one watching began to turn to see what had caused this.

"No!" I yelled.

Too late.

The vision went dark.

I held back bile.

Chapter 6

COUNCIL COLOSSUS

No, what?" Cupid shouted. "Who are you yelling at? What's happening?"

I didn't answer. I wouldn't. Cupid would have to go through this. For everyone's sake.

We landed in front of Council Colossus, the celestial city hall, and I slid off Snowlight just as Cupid and Ember touched down.

"Are you going to tell us what this is all about?!" Cupid demanded.

I narrowed my eyes his way. Though he had the right to ask, though he and Tamara hadn't earned the trouble headed their way, Cupid risked ruin if he spoke in such a tone again. *I* was safe from all to come and needn't be involved.

"Diana! Are you alright?" Tamara asked as she dropped beside Nightfall as easily as a cowgirl dropping off her Quarter Horse.

Her concern consumed her neebo. Cupid's rage consumed his, but through the pops of anger and indignation, he did finally remember I'm an oracle. He's never known about my telesthesia, my ability to know something happening elsewhere. Only my brother does. I nodded toward Tamara. "All is as it should be," I told her, which did not mean all was well, but Tamara took it as so. She remembered that the gods' concerns are many and varied, not necessarily focused on the moment.

I decided to act casual. I looked around the grounds. It was so different at night, shady and blue-black except where the building's radiance or starlight shone. And the cloudy ground offered a bit of diffused light. I ran my hands down my hips to straighten my skirt, but, really, the black leather was too thick to bunch and too short to snag on my silver hunting bow. It was great for hunting, though. And for war. I sniffed the air. It smelled … different than normal.

Tamara threaded her arms through Nightfall's black, feathered nape. "Thank you," she whispered. "I loved flying with you and hope so much to see you again." Nightfall clicked his beak in quick affection.

Cupid hoisted his leg high over Ember and shoved off. The thrust tilted Ember off balance, and she snapped at him. "Sorry," Cupid barked with palms raised. "Relax, girl. No offense meant."

Ember must have been done with him because she stomped a hind leg and took off, Nightfall and Snowlight right behind.

"Halt! Who goes there?!" rang two voices from the shadows. Before anyone could answer, a figure charged with swords in hand, bellowing a war cry.

"Janus, 'tis I, Diana, with guests Cupid and Lady

Tamara."

The figure halted in its tracks just as it stepped into a stream of light pouring from an overhead window. His stony face regarded us before shifting back into the shadows, turning around, and stepping back in, this time revealing a female face.

Tamara's neebo flashed, amazed at seeing the two-faced Celestial. *A goddess?* she thought.

How interesting. She didn't know that humans picture Janus wrong. Well, they picture him half wrong, as a male god with two faces pointing in opposite directions. Being the god of beginnings and endings, it's only natural that humans would use this particular god's face to grace coins, doorframes, gates, anything with two sides, really. But whether mortals never saw the god or they simply chose two males as a way of bolstering the patriarchy, I cannot say. Were it me having my gender erased, I'd have given those mortals no future to foresee.

Janus, the male half of the pair, guards the past and the knowledge gained from previous generations. His sister, Janice, faces the opposite way, seeing future advances and the hope of approaching generations. Their body is ambivalent, not that it's anyone's business, and they watch more abstract dualities, too, like transitions and time. So of course such a god would be bi-gender.

Janice lowered their swords, nodded, and retreated once more into the shadows.

I raised my face to Council Colossus and drew my guests' eyes toward the vainglorious superstructure before us with its pretentious splendor or, as I like to call it, its scam of sham. The CC is an elaborate, glowing building meant to exude power. It's situated just far enough from the city center to be exclusory. Although I'm a standing member of Council, along with 11 others, I rarely attend.

Cupid's thoughts were quiet; no doubt he'd seen this building before. But Tamara's mind raced with questions. Her frantic neebo bombarded my mind. Rather than attempt to defend myself from such rapid fire, I foisted the task upon her.

"Describe what you see," I commanded, "so that I might experience this through fresh eyes."

Tamara's eyes swept the expanse, and her storm of thoughts slowed as she sorted them. Her trembling neebo relaxed.

"The building's magnificent and much, much bigger than I'd have expected, considering only 12 Olympians sit at Council." *But the gods always demand more space than they need,* she thought.

I grinned, knowing that nearly all houses of government, earthly and celestial, were unnecessarily large. I've seen centuries of mortal rulers, anointed by birth, appointed by the state, or elected by the people, run their temporary fiefdoms from within these same types of marble-columned monstrosities. The sprawling buildings were usually surrounded by hyper-manicured gardens. I detest such biological orderliness, though I acknowledge that even an obedient garden is better than asphalt. The commoners summoned to these buildings by the authorities wanted to be there as little as Cupid wanted to be here now.

"I'd guess the building is six stories tall," Tamara continued, "although it's hard to say because of the columns. They're enormous. Oh, and there are 12 of them, likely to honor each council member. And look." She pointed upward. "There are statues along the roof."

"Like gargoyles," Cupid said.

I laughed. "The gargoyle Diana is third on the right." I tilted my head that direction.

Oh gods, Tamara thought.

She needn't have worried. I wasn't offended, and Cupid hadn't given it a second thought. "Go on, Tamara," I prompted.

"The, uh, the building is square with softly rounded edges. And the windows above the columns have stained glass showing, oh! historic scenes. I see now."

The light shining through the windows projected diffused images of the gods onto the cloudy ground below, the most color to be found at this time of night. As the clouds rolled, the gods contorted; their lumpy forms bulging with each watery wave.

"I think the meeting may be starting," Tamara said.

Cupid took a step forward. "Time to get on with

it. Let's crash the party."

"We were invited," Tamara reminded him. "No one will blame us for being there."

"Oh, they'll blame me, all right, when the next threat to the kingdom rears its scaly hide. You watch."

I knew the aforementioned scaly hide was continents away but rising even now. I replied the way I've often found most useful. I said nothing.

Cupid's mind pictured the whole building collapsing before he had to step inside. Meetings will do that to a person. Be still, my heart. What bravery.

Chapter 7

COUNCIL CHAMBERS

"Uh, let me get that for you ladies." Cupid grabbed the front doors' giant marble rings. "Wow, these are big as toilet seats. Fitting, as we're at the seat of government."

I laughed. Cupid smiled, then pulled the doors open with a grunt and stood back to let us pass.

Holy sickle of Saturn, thought Tamara as she followed me in and looked up.

We stood at ground level of a building in which every floor above us was transparent as glass – except for the foggy spots where Celestials stood. Their body contact frosted the transparent glass beneath them so people in the lower extremities wouldn't see, well, their lower extremities. There weren't many divine splotches gliding around at this hour. I looked back at Tamara. Her eyes had reached the top level, the only one with an opaque floor, thus breaking the view to the vaulted ceiling.

Security and secrecy in one, she thought.

Stuffy snobs, Cupid thought, and I looked over to see him also eyeing the upper chambers.

Tamara's sights drifted lower, to the glass directly above us. Her eyes followed it from the back of the building to the point it ended, a few meters short of the building's front wall. "The floor stops before the façade,"

Tamara said, "leaving a gap, as if there was once a stairwell. But it's empty now. Huh. Well, guess we fly up." She held out a hand to assist me. How thoughtful.

But those who enter these esteemed halls need never exert themselves. A miniature tornado materialized within the gap and plummeted down on top of us. Tamara cried out and shielded herself with her hands. The funnel lifted us off our feet and jetted upward. As a non-flyer, I found the spinning exhilarating. My companions struggled and bounced off the façade more than once, feathers flying. The twister rose and spit us out at the seventh floor, the bane of my existence.

Giant cedar doors before us creaked open, and Habandash poked his head out, checking for stragglers. I regretted being one. I'd have rather been an absentee.

"Ah, Diana," Habandash called in greeting. "And Cupid and Tamara!" The voice of Jupiter's executive assistant held marked surprise. "How nice of you – three – to join us. You've decided, Cupid, to begin your training?"

Cupid raised a brow, his thoughts all questions: *What training? Why does he know about this and I don't? What's going on?*

I strode into the chamber. The hard, polished cloud floor felt dreadful compared to my preferred woodland undergrowth, which was always soft and pungent with the scent of life.

"Why, Diana!" Jupiter exclaimed. "Both you and

your brother Apollo deign to attend council? On the same night? Why am I suddenly … anxious?"

The loveliest goddess in the room stepped forward. Venus put a finger under her chin.

"Well to be anxious, oh god of gods,
when seers, oft' absent, come nigh.
Oracles leading my son? His bride?
Such rare visits do mystify."

I snickered.

"Hi, Mom," Cupid said, stepping through the doorway behind Tamara and hugging his mother, the goddess of love. "Diana and Apollo are absent by choice, but *IIIIIIII've* never been invited."

Tamara, perhaps sensing offense, walked over to Venus, taking all attention with her. She began to curtsy before the goddess caught her hand and pulled her upright. Venus dropped an air kiss above Tamara's right ear. I wondered how valiantly a suitor might fight for such a kiss. Venus turned to Cupid once more.

"Dost thou come by choice, my son?
Or under a prophet's decree?
Pray, dost thou, heir declared,
master thine own destiny?"

I snickered again. I do that a lot around her. So does everyone else. Nerves, I guess.

"Very droll, Mother," Cupid said. "I think 'heir' is a pretty strong word. It's only been a few weeks since

Mercury attacked the kingdom and Jupiter said – I don't really know." He leaned in to whisper in her ear, "I actually thought he was kidding when he named me his successor. You know, caught up in the moment?" He leaned back and raised his voice to normal. "So, no, I haven't had time to learn the workings of council, much less 'master my destiny.' What does that even mean to you?"

Venus pursed her lips and oh-so-subtly flicked her eyes toward the king.

Cupid nodded at Jupiter, impatient. I thought it was a fairly enormous breach in protocol to ignore the King of Olympus, but I liked Cupid's attention to his mom, so I said nothing.

"Welcome, Cupid. Tamara," said Jupiter.

Tamara's neebo cowed. Well, Jupiter's physical attributes intimidated so many. His tall, muscled build, angular face, and startlingly blue eyes drilled into everyone. She squinted as his white robe dazzled her. I nudged her neebo to fight her instinct to curtsy and instead nod like Cupid. The heads of all the councilmembers dipped in return.

"It is time you join us," Jupiter announced, as if their being there had anything to do with him. "Apollo assures me today is a good day to start."

Start what, exactly? Cupid asked, silent as the constellations.

"I call this meeting to order," Habandash announced

while rapping a white gavel against a matching pedestal stand behind him. A familiar assistant readied a scroll and quill to take notes. I noticed it was the same red-haired member of the Fallen Four who'd greeted them at Cupid's proposal, the one they called Cornelius. Tamara sent him a grin, which he returned.

Oh gods, Cupid thought. *Governance. Just the worst.*

Each councilmember turned around to face the room's curved, outer white walls. A spot of wall in front of each of us puckered, as if someone were pinching the cooled skin off soup. The pinched sections broke away to created smooth, horizontal disks about a meter in diameter that hovered before a god. The disks then transformed to depict that god's nature.

Mine turned brown with distinct rings to mimic the cross section of a tree trunk. Woody sprouts grew upward from it. Some wove themselves into a throne upon which I sat. Others surrounded me in trees and moss. My paradise pod flourished, green and lush with roots dangling underneath. The pod swiveled to face our king.

Jupiter's platform morphed to striated marble. A throne pushed up, sizzling and popping with electricity, along with a fat column topped by a bowl. Inside it, stardust sparkled. An eagle flew down from seemingly nowhere and settled on the platform's edge.

"What should we do?" Tamara whispered to Cupid.

He shrugged and said nothing because he didn't

want to sound ignorant of Council happenings, which he absolutely was. Instead, he turned to find somewhere to sit but then noticed a white disk where the door had been. The disk hovered at knee height, then bobbed as if inviting him onto it.

I watched as it turned from white to blood red. Swirls of crimson smoke rose from the base and curled until they took shape, solidifying to form an elaborate divan. It was an alluring piece of furniture. Its heart-shaped back and armrest were edged in gold carving and looked plush and soft. Its velvety red fabric was embellished with lighter hearts of painstaking, red thread quilling. More smoke formed wine shelves stocked in reds. Still more smoke formed bellows blowing heart-shaped bubbles. And flowers. So. Many. Flowers. Red roses, pink azaleas, creamy gardenias, blue forget-me-nots, and white baby's breath. Their intoxicating smell drifted to me, and I closed my eyes in delight. The room's whole ambiance changed in an instant.

Aw crap, Cupid's thought interrupted.

"The dais recognizes your godliness," Habandash said. Cornelius scribbled furiously onto the scroll. "Mercury would normally call the meeting to order, being messenger god and secretary to the council, but as he is now, eh," – Habandash looked to Jupiter – "may I say persona non grata at the moment, sir, until you lift his punishment?"

"Yes," Jupiter said, "and his punishment includes

being replaced at Council."

No, Cupid thought. *I do NOT want to do this. And I'll never be ready for this. And Jupiter will probably forgive Mercury in a century or two and reinstate him, and here his dais recognizes my godliness, and liquid mercury can encase flowers forever.*

"Just a moment!" said a voice to our right.

Tamara's eyes immediately landed on the source of the objection, about a quarter of the way around the circle.

Make mental note, I commanded her neebo.

Minerva, Tamara thought. I felt a powerful wave of awe and fear wash over her. *The goddess of wisdom and strategy in war.*

I tried to look at Minerva the way a first time viewer might. She terrified most people, towering over them with a pale, chiseled face that looked unforgiving. I reached to gather Tamara's thoughts, but she'd noticed Minerva's famous shield, covered with lambskin and balancing on its side at her feet. There, Minerva's ever-present companion ruffled its feathers. The yellow and brown owl flapped its way onto her shoulder to claw her leather wrap. Minerva didn't flinch.

I wonder if she trained that thing, Cupid thought. *How do you train an owl?*

I felt Tamara's surprise that at Minerva's feet were baskets overflowing with weaponry. Daggers, swords, and spears lay haphazardly. *Jupiter allows weapons in Council*

Chambers? Tamara thought. I commended her. It was a fair question considering Minerva's history.

Then Tamara looked at Minerva's armor and shivered. The armor was made entirely from Jupiter's gristle. Tamara remembered the story: Jupiter was prophesied to be overthrown by one of his children. To prevent the prophecy coming true, Jupiter swallowed his pregnant mistress. She and their unborn daughter survived, and Minerva was born inside him.

Jupiter's angry lover forged armor from his gut and taught Minerva the ways of war. The constant clanging and ringing gave Jupiter an excruciating headache, so he called for his son, Vulcan, to somehow help Apollo peer into his head and cure him.

Vulcan short-cutted the project. Without warning, he swung and buried an axe into Jupiter's head, cleaving his skull in two. Out of this "splitting headache" popped Minerva, armored and armed.

"Let us be clear," Minerva demanded. "Cupid is here for induction into council, not ascendancy, as wild rumors suggest."

The gods murmured. Tamara leaned in toward Cupid. "Honey?" she whispered and I heard through her neebo. "Do you want to be inducted into council?"

Cupid shook his head.

"Then why aren't you protesting?"

"Because I won't crumple in front of my father," he

whispered back.

"But Mars Senior—"

"Thinks I'm a pansy, and if I back out of this supposedly elite gig I'll only confirm it."

Minerva raised her hands for attention. "I move we keep Mercury's position empty, leaving the council with 11 members and removing the possibility of tied votes."

"Mine is always the deciding vote," Jupiter reminded her. "And despite the *headache* an even number can cause," – he paused for the chuckles that broke out – "more voices in the council are better than fewer. That is *fairest*, wouldn't you agree?"

Venus snorted with laughter. Minerva's eyes flicked her way.

Tamara looked to Venus' clamshell dais. Few know that Venus reflects everyone's ideal feminine beauty, thus becoming beautiful to all. I let my curiosity win and see Tamara's ideal. Hers was an olive-skinned Latina with flowing black hair and a powerful stance. She carried a bow made of concentrated blue-white light. My Venus was athletic and deep brown, like the women warriors of African Dahomey. Her black hair was pulled back under a headscarf, and she always carried a dagger, tucked into her waistband, to defend her nation.

Tamara looked across the circle to Mars, Venus' lover. The god of war stared at Venus wolfishly. I could have peeked through the neebo I'd implanted in Mars and the rest of Council millennia ago – everyone loves flowers – but I knew I'd detest his thoughts. I went back to Tamara, who noticed that Mars' Roman armor didn't have any of the caked viscera from the last time she'd seen him, but the base of his dais was all debris as if a bomb had gone off under his feet. Everything there was splattered in blood. Tamara steered her eyes up along the spears and javelins to a cloud curtain behind him projecting active battle scenes. *Like a movie screen,* she thought, *only it's real. Humans somewhere on Earth fighting other humans. As if they don't have enough problems.*

"Minerva fears competition," Venus sassed.

Tamara remembered the story behind Minerva and Venus' animosity. She pictured a wedding banquet, lovely and grand, except for a goddess lurking at the edges. Eris, the goddess of discord, was of course not invited and thus became determined to spread misery. She tossed into the crowd a golden apple inscribed "To the fairest." Amazingly, only three goddesses claim it: Juno, Minerva, and Venus. Jupiter wasn't foolish enough to decide the apple's ownership, so he enlisted Paris, a fair-minded mortal, to pick the winner.

Each goddess offered a bribe. Juno dangled riches. Minerva offered wisdom and skill in war. But clever Venus tempted him with the world's most beautiful woman. I can only conclude that Paris was delirious from the sight of three goddesses at once because he foolishly accepted

Venus' gift. He received Helen, whom he stole off to Troy and whose Spartan husband set sail to retrieve. So the Judgment of Paris changed history and triggered the decade-long Trojan War.

Venus won that bet and had been rubbing it in ever since. She sang,

> "A wager so major
> judged by a teenager
> could never be won by thee.
> For Paris, sweet Paris,
> bewitched by the fairest,
> chose Helen as proxy for me."

Mars bellowed in laughter.

Minerva raised a spear.

"Ladies!" Jupiter interjected – with a clap of thunder for effect.

"Finally, some noise and outrage in this chamber!" Bacchus exulted with a gleeful spin, nearly tripping over the ceramic skulls on his dais, some of his many stage props. He had rhinestone tiaras and fishnet stockings draped over a tall mirror. Intertwined vines waved at his perceived audience while bunches of grapes tipped out of an overflowing bowl, suggesting drink.

Gods help us, thought Cupid.

"Let's cast Cupid into this production," Bacchus continued. "He's not as villainous or treacherous as Mercury, but he'll make for a fine dramatic lead."

"Dramatic lead?!" Minerva asked from across the circle.

"Did I say lead?" asked Bacchus with a grin. "I meant understudy."

Tamara noticed that the dais next to Bacchus was empty, as were two others. She processed their owners in a flash.

Neptune, still at sea. His dais was made of the sea's rolling waves supporting a blue and pink coral throne. Behind it hung a curtain of seawater shrouding dark shadows shaped like sharks.

Ceres, goddess of the harvest. Her dais of golden grains, speckled with wildflowers, swayed in a gentle breeze. Her throne was cobbled together from ancient tools of cultivation. Four sickle blades crisscrossed to form the seat. Two wooden waterwheels formed the sides. And the back was made of stretched mesh, no doubt used to separate the wheat from the chaff.

Oh wow, Tamara thought. *Vulcan.* His throne was made of red metal joined by silver plates and grommets. The back rose and split into "horns" of various metals and stones and crystals. Lava churned all around it. *He's probably at his lair.*

I always wondered if Vulcan hated being at council because it put him near the parents who abandoned him and the brother who covets his wife.

"Minerva is correct that three cast members are

absent," Bacchus cooed. "Yet the walk-ons of Diana and Apollo do add mystery."

"Yes," Juno said, stabbing the air with a wrinkled finger. "Enough suspense. Explain."

She's a prickly one, Tamara thought. *I'd use much harsher words.*

Juno, our queen, turned grey over eons of hunting down the hundreds of illegitimate children born of her playboy husband-slash-brother. My chaste lifestyle appeases her. But my brother's pastime of sexual conquests – male or female – remind her far too much of her own burden of a mate. I wondered how Juno, as goddess of marriage and the state, tolerated Jupiter's womanizing with diplomacy and grace – until her neebo clued me in. She genuinely loves him. What an awful condition.

"Diana and I are often absent because we choose to let others lead," Apollo said.

Juno squinted and said, "Those who fail to partake in governance forfeit consent in how they're governed. Regardless, let's move on."

"I motion we induct Cupid into the council!" Bacchus shouted, although no one said the matter was up for a vote.

Everybody say no, Cupid pleaded in his mind.

"Seconded already!" Juno blared.

I should've let the griffin eat me, Cupid thought.

"All in favor," Habandash called, "say aye."

Cupid's and Tamara's eyes shot around the chamber at the same moment as mine, and I saw three perspectives at once through the neebo. The vertigo nauseated me, but it did allow me to take it all in.

Six gods said aye: Venus; Apollo and me, as it was our plan to get Cupid here; Bacchus because of how much this would irk Minerva and his constant search for drama (although I also sensed a lingering loyalty for Cupid, having given him his latest adventure and a reprieve from perpetual boredom); Mars for the same reasons, not at all for familial loyalty; and Jupiter, who would obviously support what he felt was his idea.

Cornelius scribbled like mad. Beads of sweat dotted his fluffy hairline.

"All opposed, say nay," Habandash called.

"Nay," said Minerva. Juno was silent.

I felt something happen. I felt bodies stirring, one freezing in shock like the capuchin monkey from earlier. And then – oh! Earth itself moved. I looked to Apollo, who watched me closely. We turned toward Jupiter and said in unison, "Your majesty, please check your ERP."

Chapter 8

IMPACT

Jupiter narrowed his eyes before reaching into the high-standing bowl at his side. He grabbed a handful of stardust and flung it onto the floor, which rippled to reveal nighttime Earth. The CC floor is the largest Earthly Reflecting Pool in the kingdom.

I'm sure Jupiter spied on the mortal world with some regularity, perhaps scouting for beautiful ladies to deflower. And I'm convinced that the world normally looked fairly peaceful except for the regularity of war happening somewhere or other at any given time. But this was no peace we witnessed below. Even by the ERP's night vision, we could see smoke billow from a seaside port of East India. What was once a fishing community was now flattened steel and concrete. Grand houses and pitiable huts were equally crushed or toppled. Their surviving residents stood outside in pajamas, dazed.

My heart ached for them.

The destruction trailed inland, heading north-northwest. We gods leaned forward to see a giant striding across vast expanses, over hills and toward the plains skirting the Himalaya Mountains. The giant stopped to scoop the debris it created and added the mess to its armor. I looked closer. Its armor was made of scores of flattened metal shipping containers, the kind stacked on cargo ships. The containers were joined by bending their edges together, the way a child might crinkle aluminum foil to shape it. Wedged between cracks in the behemoth's armor were uprooted trees and the recently deceased, animal and human alike.

Venus covered her mouth.

Look at that, thought Mars. *What size advantage. Stupendous.*

Bacchus was the first to speak, confirming what we all dreaded. "A Primordial." He sounded fascinated. "It's loose."

Jupiter leapt off his dais to a horrendous crash of thunder. "HOW IS A PRIMORDIAL LOOSE?!" he roared.

No one dared answer despite their thousand thoughts assaulting me. I closed my eyes to focus on Cupid and Tamara alone. She leaned in and whispered, "I thought the Primordials were legend."

"We wish," he whispered in answer. "They're the oldest and wildest gods. They don't even have what we'd think of as normal bodies. They're more like a gelling of emotion or time, like the goddess Nyx, who's nighttime personified. That's why that one is adding stuff to itself. It's creating a body with debris. Anyway, Primordials sprung up during The Chaos, the time before any of us knew what the universe was. They produced the Titans, our ancestors, who were slightly less whackadoodle. But we Olympians still had to fight them, too, and toss their crazy butts in the clink."

Bolts of electricity popped off Jupiter's head like a short-circuiting plasma ball. He was shouting something about jailbreaks.

Cupid continued, "Anyway, most of the Primordials and Titans were imprisoned in Tartarus, well below The Underworld that you saw, Tamara. It's a much worse place."

Tamara shivered. Bacchus noticed and leaned over to listen in.

"Tartarus is where we keep people for eternity," Cupid said. "It's where Jupiter sent Prometheus for giving fire to mortals. That wasn't such a bad thing in itself, but Prometheus stole the fire from Jupiter, so now Prometheus is tied down there, getting his liver eaten every day by Jupiter's eagle, only to suffer the pain of having it regrow every night. Tartarus is the place we send people we want to forget."

"And you can bet, my dear," chimed in Bacchus in a hush, "that anyone escaping that prison will be out for sweet revenge."

He smiled, and Tamara frowned.

Jupiter turned back to his dais, reached for more stardust, and threw the new batch down. The surface revealed a scene of horror few could attest to seeing: The Underworld in its typical and awful glory.

Aw, hell, Cupid thought.

Tamara's nausea sickened even her neebo.

The floor felt insubstantial as we watched thousands of blackened souls in The Underworld scramble across sinking sands, desperate to escape fire-breathing dragons. The raging beasts charred many of the hopeful escapees and bit down on stragglers – but didn't eat them – so that they fell wounded and in pain to scramble anew. The dragons swung their horned tails to throw other victims far and wide.

The souls converged toward a wall made of three parts. The lowest section was mud, up to the height of an average man. The middle section was red adobe brick and ran a few meters taller. Finally, the top section was solid gold. Dangling over the top of the wall were full, green branches weighted down with bright, bursting fruit, promising sweet relief. Beyond those branches, on the other side of the wall, spread a green field teeming with life, bathed in gentle shade.

Those poor, wretched souls who reached the wall scraped their fingers raw trying to purchase grip on the mud, but, each time they did, the mud reverted to dry soil that slid through their fingers. It was unclimbable but did not topple.

The souls who managed to leap higher, over the mud, burnt their fingertips on the hot adobe brick.

Those clever few who tried to outwit the game,

who climbed on the shoulders of a partner to reach the golden top, sunk together as a pair into the desert sands at their feet and arose again behind the dragons.

"Pluto!" Jupiter bellowed. "Show yourself!"

The god of The Underworld materialized front and center, gaunt and grim, and, as usual, displeased.

"After our last brotherly quarrel, in the Colosseum, you demanded that I return to the work of managing the dead – and now, so soon after, you interrupt?" asked Pluto with plain hostility. "I am busy today punishing the greedy with eternal want." He scanned the room and spotted Tamara. "As theft from The Underworld constitutes greed, and you, Protected Miss, stole not merely a coin from my kitchen but also the affections of my pet, perhaps you'd like to join us."

"You son of a –" Cupid started.

"Be careful what you call my mother, Cupid," Juno interrupted. "Pluto's mother is also my own."

"And mindest thou, Pluto, whom thou dost threaten," Venus said, tilting her dais toward the lord of darkness. "Tamara belongs not in thy foul world."

Mom throws some shade, Cupid thought.

Tamara swallowed hard, her neebo transmitting gratitude.

Pluto turned a deadly glare toward the goddess of love.

Venus returned the glare tenfold, adding,

"Much lava flows beneath the ground,
    bubbling, boiling, round and round.
My husband, king of lava crowned,
    guides its flow, LEST YE be drowned."

The purgatory far behind Pluto burst into flames, and its inhabitants writhed in agony. Pluto cocked his head her way.

She answered,

"Hurt thine own. What do I care?
They feel no love. They're dead. So there."

Bacchus burst out laughing.

Pluto turned a stony gaze his way.

"Stop this nonsense," demanded Jupiter. "A Primordial is loose. Explain yourself."

Pluto looked from face to face to ascertain the joke. He smoothed his own pale countenance. "That cannot be. I check every night. And I do so alone to keep the path to Tartarus secret."

"How did you not hear or feel it leave, Pluto?" Jupiter asked, doubting.

Pluto breathed slowly out his nose, as if cooling himself after an insult. "Unlike so many gods, I actually work. In a grim place. With a grim task."

Jupiter waved a hand to silence him before we again had to hear his woe-is-me tirade. "Continue with that work," Jupiter commanded, grabbing more stardust, "but send forces to recapture it." Jupiter threw the dust onto the floor before Pluto could protest. The Primordial moving on Earth reappeared.

Apollo leaned forward. The herds of beasts roaming in the far distance of his dais lowed, and sheet music near his sandaled feet spilled to the floor. "You had warning of this attack, Your Majesty," Apollo said. "The Fates' prophesy."

"What?" Jupiter sneered. "I don't listen to those old hags."

"My sister and I also warned you," Apollo said, "and we are no hags."

Juno cleared her throat. "What prophesy is this?"

I had half a mind to dissect her with an arrow, seeing as how she spent decades hunting my brother and me for her husband's indiscretions with our mother. But adulthood requires deplorable tolerance.

"The prophesy of consequences," Apollo said.

"Is this why you're here?" she asked, turning to me. "Did you foresee an attack and do nothing to stop it?"

I gestured toward Cupid as proof indeed that I did something to stop it.

Why are they looking at me? Cupid asked himself. *I didn't cause this.*

"Welcome to governance, Cupid," Bacchus cooed.

Cupid squeezed his eyes together and held back a hateful string of thoughts that no one but I could hear.

A scream from outside opened his eyes.

"Go away!" screamed the voice.

"Stay here!" Cupid said to Tamara. He ran toward the wall where they'd come in. The wall opened a hole for him. I'd never seen it do that before.

Tamara followed, but the hole sealed itself behind Cupid. She ran headlong into the wall and fell back with a thud.

Bacchus hopped off his dais and put a hand under her elbow to help her up. He brought her closer and whispered, "My dear, it would not do to disobey the gods right in their council chambers. Please stay here as was requested."

As was ordered, Tamara corrected in her thoughts, but her neebo transmitted respect toward Bacchus. She nodded.

I dropped off my dais, and Apollo and I went through the door to assist Cupid. We knew where we were going and what we'd see. When we reached the plaza outside, we found Cupid stepping away from a figure with his palms out. When he saw me, he explained, "They're … turned to stone."

"HE'S turned!" Janice shouted. "I'M trapped! Help me!"

Apollo and I walked around her. Janus was calcified.

"She'll come back!" Janice cried. "But I can't leave. How can I avoid her?"

"Avoid who?" asked Cupid. "Who did this?"

"I… I couldn't see, thank the gods, but I heard … rattling and hissing. I think … oh, gods." She shifted her eyes as if trying to move her head, which wouldn't budge. Her features contorted in desperation. "I think it was a Gorgon!"

Chapter 9

AVERSION

A Gorgon?" Cupid asked. "Like Medusa? That's…" *ridiculous*, he thought. "Impossible. There were only three Gorgons. Two haven't been seen since Medusa was killed by Perseus ages ago. Maybe he killed them, too, for all we know, but if the Gorgons had children before they died – snakelets?"

"They would not have snakelets," I said. "They would have had mortal children or half-gods. They were human before the curse."

"Well, the legends say Medusa bore some cooky creatures," Cupid said, "like the winged horse Pegasus and a giant that sprang from her body after she was beheaded. As for the other Gorgons, who knows what they might have birthed?"

I narrowed my eyes at him, but he didn't notice, deep in thought as he was. He walked around Janice to see Janus' face. He leaned in, and his neebo showed me what he saw: the aged face of a person who always looks to the past. That face was contorted in fear, the eyebrows raised to impossible heights, the eyes wide enough to see the whites all around. Well, you might have been able to see the whites if any color were discernible within rock. Janus' stretched mouth was presumably caught mid-scream, the last sound he'd ever make. Cupid tapped Janus' petrified cheek twice with his index finger. The thwunk-thwunk sound reminded him of his limo driving over seams in pavement.

Who could have done this? Cupid thought while pressing down on Janus' ossified shoulders as if trying to trigger an undo button. *Couldn't be a Gorgon. But their offspring? Who would want to mate with a Gorgon anyway?*

I bristled at his insensitivity.

"Whatever their offspring might be, if they had any," Cupid continued, "they'd be hiding away, on the other side of the world. What's the name of that island the Gorgons settled?" he asked, straightening up to look at me. "Off the coast of South America, wasn't it?"

"Isla Gorgona," I answered pointedly, "a wild and dangerous place now famed for its venomous snakes. Of course, Medusa was the one who drew them there."

"Right. Well, the island was supposedly rocky and uninviting, and she was a hermit who wanted nothing to do with people from all I've heard, so it sounds like she found the right place to repel people."

"You make it sound like she had a choice," I said. "She was not in favor with the gods, and to be in the company of humans meant killing them, so she exiled herself, yes, but not at all by choice."

"Why are you defending her?" Cupid asked. He shook his head. "This is off topic. Medusa's dead. The other Gorgons, maybe not."

"*Someone* turned my brother to stone – *and* trapped me in our body!" Janice wailed. "Doooo something!" She sobbed but could not lift a hand to wipe her tears.

A rattle broke through her grief.

"It's back!" she wailed.

The ch-ch-ch-chiiiiiii snapped Cupid to attention. The sound lingered in the air before more rattles joined it, creating a collective chirring that grew in intensity. The nighttime air spoiled with a new, musky stench.

"Holy hydra," Cupid said.

"A hydra would have only one tail," I corrected.

Cupid frowned at me before walking back around the pair. "Janice, with your brother turned to stone, you're too heavy for me to lift and get out of here."

She whimpered.

"But I can make a water ball around you, and the buoyancy will make you lighter. Then I can try rolling you into the CC."

"I'll drown!"

"You'll be fine," Cupid assured her and waved an arm. Ribbons of water pulled away from the surrounding clouds and wrapped around her, covering her layer by layer, leaving her head free. She wouldn't drown.

Hissing rose all around us, sinister and venomous, suspending our thoughts.

Better get rolling, he thought and readied himself

to tip her over and roll her sideways. He'd just set a leg back to prepare for the push when I felt a change in air pressure. I felt an onslaught headed our way and looked up to see a barrage of long, thin shapes soaring toward us.

"Incoming!" Apollo and I shouted together. We shielded ourselves with our hands, but the torrent of leathery coils pelted us anyway, scraping our arms and legs.

Janice screamed. We lowered our arms to see a mottled black and white cobra wrapped around her head. It opened its hood.

"What the – " Cupid said.

"Nooooooo-!" Janice screamed, and we watched in horror as she turned to stone right before our eyes. The cobra bared its fangs and struck, too late. It dropped to the ground, unconscious from ramming against solid rock.

Cupid stared at it a moment, stunned. A heartbeat later he thrust out his arms. The water surrounding Janice flew outward to create a water bubble around us. We had four meters of space in any direction before we touched water. I admit that I got momentarily lost in the beauty of standing within a water sphere, the liquid swirling and blurring the world around us, and so I heard Cupid's neebo too late. He'd followed Janice's eyes and saw what she'd seen. A shape swayed just outside the water, its features made blurry.

It took just a few moments for him to realize that the figure was much larger than any of us and had no legs.

Its lower half was a bright green, serpentine coil. The body was that of a woman – or what had once been – jet black from waist to clavicle. The face was mostly black but lightened subtly to dark green at her hairline – only there was no hair. Instead of feminine, curly locks, this creature was crowned with writhing snakes. The twisting forms suddenly faced him. I imagined the Gorgon's legendary eyes as vertical slits of neon green. Were they still trained on Janice or watching us behind Cupid's water veil?

So many thoughts circled his mind, Cupid could only settle on saying, "She's armed."

I looked again through the blear. She'd reached a hand over her shoulder to pull an arrow out of an unseen quiver. Her other hand held a large bow extended in warning. Two short-handled sledgehammers hung on chains at her hips. Her impressive armor included a bronze breastplate and segmented scales extending down her tail.

Cupid asked no one in particular, "Is – is that a Gorgon?"

"You seriously don't know?" Apollo answered.

"If I'd've seen one before, I'd be dead," he retorted with a frown. He turned his face back toward her. "Why hasn't she come through the water?"

"Maybe she didn't expect the water to distort her image. Maybe it's lucky you're alive. Maybe she'll figure it out and come through yet," I said.

Cupid looked at me open-mouthed, aghast. "We

need to get inside," he urged. "Apollo, you're a healer. If we move the Jani, can you help them?"

Apollo's eyes glowed before he answered, "Their future is uncertain. I see us inside without them. Come." He rolled his hands and gathered light. He directed the rays outward to create a blinding space around us and a tunnel straight ahead.

"Keep your eyes on your feet," I advised as we headed back to Council Colossus. But even with our eyes trained, we spotted thin black shadows out of the corners of our eyes. They approached us only to catch fire.

"You told Jupiter about a prophecy," Cupid said as we walked.

"The same one you received," I replied.

"Uh, no. Tamara and I haven't seen The Fates lately, so no creepy prophecies, thank the gods."

"The Fates speak in many ways."

Tamara's face materialized in Cupid's mind. She stood in Cupid Castle in front of a wall of shelves piled high with scrolls. The opposite side of that room featured a bank of windows overlooking an expanse of lawn leading to a pond. I sensed that their dog, Cerberus, and Bacchus' panthers had fought at that pond.

The scrolls, Cupid thought with exhaustion, tired of the issue and frustrated with Tamara's insistence that he read them, that they must mean something, and why were they being delivered to him via spiders of all things.

Didn't he see that as ominous? she'd asked.

No, he'd said. *If The Fates didn't want to deliver their message in person, that was just fine with him. So of course the hags would be nasty and employ a spider the size of a rabbit. And that spider would definitely look smooth as black glass and would obviously weave a parachute web to catch the wind to travel more quickly. And then it would certainly crouch its way into the castle and creep its twitchy, crawly self over to me and walk on my face as I slept, as spiders do. And it would love to feel my muscles tighten as it dropped a scroll on my forehead and glared into my two eyes with its eight. It makes sense. The Fates are weavers, too. Nona spins the thread of life, her sister Decima measures it, and Morta cuts it at life's end. Nothing odd about any of it.*

Cupid continued to play the scene in his mind. "You're ignoring the messages," Tamara had fretted. *But if the message was important*, Cupid had thought to himself, *The Fates would show up in person. They'd appear as crones, gaunt to the point of death, or budding beauties or jump-roping little girls and then talk in cryptic rhymes as if anyone could understand their warnings ahead of time. No, it was only after the world nearly ended that you'd figure out what they meant. It's all so much drama. Those three biddies should hang out with Bacchus...*

And I should have read the scrolls, Cupid thought to himself.

Yes, I thought, you should have.

Chapter 10

SIEGE

The CC doors were wide open. The second we passed the threshold, Cupid slammed the doors shut and ran to the nearest window. He yanked the curtains off the rod and sprinted toward the door, dropping to a knee slide to tuck the fabric into the crannies underneath.

"Sons of mortals!" Cupid cussed. "This building isn't airtight." He looked up. "Tamara."

Cupid didn't wait for the funnel to take him up. He spread his big, blue-tipped wings and shot upward to council chambers. Apollo wrapped an arm around my shoulders and launched us up together so I wouldn't have to wait for the lift.

"There you are!" we heard Tamara say as we stepped into the chamber. "You won't believe what's happening," she said, pointing behind her.

Jupiter grabbed a thunderbolt that materialized beside his throne. As its light pulsed, the edges of the room shadowed like a brownout, as if there was only so much power to go around. Jupiter took aim and hurled the bolt through the ERP to Earth. I got the impression he'd been firing bolts since we left the room. I leaned forward to watch the charge electrify the Primordial. It struck true, but the creature seemed more enraged than hurt. It howled and raised a fist to the heavens before reaching down and scooping some of the hundreds of serpents slithering its way. It reached back like a baseball pitcher and hurled the legless slinks up to the heavens. A moment later we heard the thup-thup-thup of snakes striking the building.

"Your Highness," Cupid said, looking around in alarm, "the giant isn't our only problem. Olympus is being attacked. Janice gave us what warning she could, but we need to fortify this building until we can figure out what's going on. My water wall isn't going to work. Snakes are great swimmers, and I'd bet so are Gorgons."

"Gorgons?" Minerva asked with furrowed brow.

"Yes, Gorgons!" Cupid barked. "Keep up, Minerva!"

Tamara gasped, and before Jupiter could rev his next bolt, a spear soared across the chamber and ran Cupid through.

"Cupid!" Tamara screamed as he fell back. She lunged toward him.

"If you lay a hand upon that god," Minerva warned, stopping Tamara dead in her tracks, "I shall make those commoner appendages of yours decay to bone."

Tamara stepped back slowly, her eyes to the ground. *Sociopath,* she thought to herself. Only when she'd steadied herself at Bacchus' side once again did she look up – to Mars, god of war, counterpart to Minerva as its goddess. The side of his mouth tilted into a grin.

Love a good girl fight, he thought to himself. Darn.

I usually tried tuning out his neebo.

Cupid rolled onto an elbow and clutched his gut. "Gods dammit, Minerva. Are you nuts? You nearly killed me."

"She could've if she'd've tried," Mars said. "I've seen her pierce a bison's heart at a quarter mile."

Bacchus grinned. Drama was drama, no matter the cause.

"You will address me with proper respect," Minerva warned Cupid, "unless you'd like me as an enemy."

Juno's dais slid forward. "And you, Minerva, will kindly respect these chambers."

I was wondering when the goddess of state would intervene. She can't let governing gods just go around lancing each other.

"The immediate need is fortification," she went on, wagging a finger toward the door, "against snakes particularly. As we're figuring that out, Apollo, would you please tend to Cupid's injury?" She looked at Cupid with pursed lips. "I'm sure he's learned his lesson."

Apollo bent and pulled up Cupid by his once-white but now blood-soaked shirt. Apollo pinched Cupid's open wound with one hand and used his other hand's index finger to create a laser beam that cauterized the cut. Cupid's neebo whimpered and wailed, but Cupid himself set his jaw and didn't flinch. His wound disappeared as Apollo stood.

"Diiiiiiiiana," Juno sang with glee. "It appears you finally have a use. You can talk to animals. I suppose it's a way for you to commune with your own kind."

Even Bacchus blanched at the insult from the goddess who'd just requested respect.

I closed my eyes and vacillated between rage and answering coolly. "Would 'my own kind' be the half of me that comes from Jupiter and relates to carnality?"

"Hoo HOO!" Bacchus crowed.

"Grandma, stop spoiling for a fight," Cupid said, getting to his feet and still rubbing his gut. He lifted his chin toward Minerva. "This butcher's affecting you."

Before Minerva finished clenching the hilt of her sword, Cupid whipped his hand over his shoulder, set his arrow, and fired her way. I gasped at his speed. I hadn't detected his plan. Even his neebo were catching up. The arrow whizzed within an inch of Minerva's left hip and disappeared into the fresh darkness created by yet another of Jupiter's thunderbolts. I expected to hear a skid of arrowhead against polished floor. Instead I heard an anguished hiss and the scrape of squirming scales.

Jupiter released his bolt, and the room lit anew. Cupid had skewered a viper. Turquoise blue. It would have been gorgeous in its natural habitat. Another reptile rose behind it, yellow and black with jagged scales. Minerva threw a knife that I guessed she hid within her clothes because I hadn't seen her reach for it. It cut into the viper's neck and stabbed it into place on the wall behind her. It reminded me of a hanging kitchen spoon.

"We've got to secure this place," Cupid said, turning to face me. "I don't know what we can do yet against the Gorgons, but snakes are literally raining down on us – and crawling into the building. Diana, can you send them away?"

"Yes, Cupid, indeed I could influence the snakes, but I rarely command an animal to behave against its will. It would cost me their trust and thus much of my natural domain."

Lunatics, he thought. *All these gods are wackos.*

"Besides, the snakes leaving won't fix the problem, Cupid," I continued, "only delay a grander one. I am a seer, and my sight turns black if today's poison is pushed to the future."

"What do you mean "your sight turns black?" Jupiter asked.

"I mean I see no future."

"That can't be," Jupiter said with a sneer.

His doubt of my vision cut like claws. I looked to the door, where shapes dappled the light leaking underneath.

"Apollo," Jupiter asked, "is this our end?"

Apollo's eyes glowed a mere fraction before he said, "All ends are a beginning. All beginnings are an end."

Jupiter frowned. He reached over to the staff at

his side, lifted it, and struck it down against his dais. The impact boomed. The hair on my arms rose with the popping and zizzing of a thousand electric charges. White light pulsed outside, and I imagined the skyfire would have cut off our view of the stained glass were we still standing in the plaza. We were sealed within.

What about the other Olympians? Tamara thought. *And the mortals?*

"Jupiter," Juno asked, "how will we fight if we barricade ourselves?"

A wailing alarm rose from far away, no doubt triggered by Jupiter's Royal Security Force. Cornelius dropped the scroll in his hand and looked to Habandash, who nodded. Cornelius rushed to the wall and pushed a spot that looked like any other but revealed a hidden compartment. He grabbed a notepad within and slashed his quill across sheet after sheet before tossing them into the air, where they disappeared with a pop. "Fortify. Gorgons attacking," he'd written. Notes with dire warnings went out to every Olympian household.

Bacchus cleared his throat and raised a Shakespearean hand toward Minerva. "Well now, as we council members are safe backstage, how about you relay the fantastical tale of the Gorgons? It's a heartbreaking tragedy in which you, Minerva, played a starring role, but, from the looks of things, we may not know the entire story. Care to share any new, critical information?"

Chapter 11

ADVANTAGE

Minerva didn't spear *Bacchus*. I imagine his longer time in the council earned him some latitude. Instead, Minerva looked to Jupiter, and his nod left her no option but to answer.

"You know the story," Minerva said with a wave of her hand. "Medusa was a disciple in my temple. She boasted of her beauty and seduced Neptune – as if drawing Neptune's eye is any big accomplishment. The problem came when the saucy little mortal wanted her tryst to be where she imagined herself on equal footing with the gods, that is, in my temple, a spot she felt befit her rank. She and Neptune copulated at the base of my statue, right beneath my feet. Can you believe she dared such an atrocity? I could hear their raspy breath below me and smell their wanton passion floating up to my nostrils. And may I say that, when I looked down, more than once Neptune caught my eye. He actually hoped I'd see the blasphemy."

"Wait, wait, wait," Bacchus said. "Neptune watched you eye him while he bumped uglies with your disciple?" He brought his hand, limp wristed, to his chest in feigned shock.

That guy is too much, Cupid thought.

"And so," Minerva continued in her own saucy tone,

"I cursed Medusa so that none could look upon her again without turning to stone. I turned her shiny, curly locks into snakes. I made her flawless, silky skin scaly, and I transformed her lithe, nubile body into the snake she was within. I did the same for her two meddling sisters."

"So let me get this straight," Bacchus said, rubbing his middle fingers over his temples as if smoothing a migraine. "Neptune schtoops a girl. You don't like the chosen location of said banging, so you curse her – and her sisters. Am I right so far?"

Minerva stood like stone herself.

"Tamara," Bacchus said.

Oh no, she thought. *Don't pull me into this.*

"You're somewhat of an outsider, although hopefully not for long as you've helped save this kingdom not once but twice. Still, you haven't been raised in this theatre. What are your initial thoughts to this story?"

Don't answer, she thought to herself. *Pretend you don't hear. Pretend to faint. Do faint.*

Cupid tensed. I tensed. I sensed that Tamara's silence, while wise in the moment, would forever harm her standing with the council. I was about to push her neebo to urge her to speak when she did so herself.

"With due respect to the goddess," Tamara said, dipping her head Minerva's way, "I wonder why she didn't punish Neptune the same way – or any way from what I've heard."

Bacchus leapt from his dais to shield Tamara just as Cupid did the same. They crashed into each other and fumbled to regain their footing, but they made an effective wall should any lances or maces fly Tamara's way. It was Venus, however, who moved next. She raised a hand, and all eyes shot her way as usual. She said,

"'Tis a question many ask,
if mind and heart be true.
Ye cursed the lass on Neptune's brass.
Yet she, harassed, was quite outclassed,
her virtue forced adieu."

Steel would melt under the glare that Minerva shot Venus.

"I heard the same," Bacchus said. "Picture the scene. The girl is innocent but cursed with beauty. She's hounded by suitors and the unrelenting attention of Neptune. Not even the temple grounds can protect her from his desire. The story I heard, Minerva, is that Medusa was raped in your temple crying out to you for help, but she received no pity. It's said that you, out of jealousy and rage and even at that moment threatened by her beauty, turned the still-bleeding and crying girl into a monster."

My premonition kicked in. I felt how the air would split in the wake of Minerva's sword. I looked at Mars the moment Minerva's blade moved. I urged his neebo to intersect. As my eyes caught the glint of Minerva's weapon flying through the air toward Bacchus, my eyes also spotted the rotation of Mars' hatchet flying directly at me. The hatchet head clanked against her sword, deflecting both. The sword missed Bacchus by a foot, and the hatchet missed me by an inch. I didn't move.

Tamara leaned around Bacchus to stare at me. I felt her suspicion.

Mars lowered his throwing hand and said, "While I admire your fighting instinct, Minerva, and I sometimes wouldn't mind seeing that sharp tongue of Bacchus' sliced clean off, we're in a battle now, so we need intel. Tell us how it is that snakeladies are at our door if you gave Perseus the tools and your blessings to kill them?"

"She wasn't the only one," Cupid added.

A sound like the pounding of rain had us look to the stained glass window. Plops and sizzles. More snakes pouring down.

Cupid turned on his heel to address Tamara. "Several gods gave Perseus weapons to kill Medusa. You know the story, don't you, ma chère?" I got the impression his exposition wasn't really addressed to her but rather the room at large.

"Perseus wanted to harness Medusa's deadliness to kill not only the king hounding his mother but also the letch's royal guards. At some point he or someone else figured, 'why bother convincing Medusa herself when you can just take her head and travel light?'"

Tamara winced.

Cupid turned and moseyed, nonchalant, with his hands behind his back, to Minerva's dais. I thought it extremely unwise to get near so petulant a god, but Cupid played the innocent. He brought a hand forward to rub his chin, as if deep in thought. His neebo were a scramble of ideas.

Bacchus grinned and pulled away from Tamara to shadow him. Together they ambled a circle around Minerva, forcing her to shift her gaze and even look over her shoulder to keep an eye on them.

Keeping her off her game, Mars thought. *Surrounding her. Great bully ploy.*

I huffed, furious that Mars' vile thoughts kept invading my head, but he had an especially forceful aura about him that required constant deflection.

"Let's go down the list," Cupid said, resting one index finger on another. "Mercury gave Perseus winged sandals, didn't he? The same sandals Pip wears now?"

Bacchus nodded furiously.

"You know, Minerva, Mercury isn't someone you want to be lumped in with lately, he being the most recent god to try to overthrow the kingdom."

Bacchus mimed a kick as banishment. Minerva's eyes squeezed into slits.

"Then there's Pluto," Cupid continued, "the jailor who's supposed to guard Olympus' worst criminals in The Underworld. He gave Perseus the helm of darkness to make him invisible."

Wish we were invisible right now, Tamara thought.

Bacchus brought a hand to his brow as if searching the distance. I followed his eyes to see Mars picking at a nail with a kris dagger. As the wavy iron blade surely made manicuring difficult, Mars must have been waiting for the accusations to turn to blows.

Cupid stopped in front of Minerva and looked up at her on her dais. "And you, Minerva, you gave Perseus the polished shield to see Medusa's reflection."

Bacchus acted out the hunt, holding an imaginary shield in front of his face while walking backward.

"That was key to the whole thing, wasn't it? Perseus needed to see her reflection *only* – not see her face directly – to not turn to stone. Then he'd use the sword to cut off her head – and the heads of her sisters too."

Bacchus swung an imaginary sword behind his back and raised his spurious shield in victory.

"Foolish theatrics aside," Minerva said, causing Bacchus to lower his faux shield, "you tell the tale as so."

"Then why did I see a Gorgon behind my water wall, Minerva?" Cupid asked.

Juno's dais lurched forward. "You, you saw one?!"

"Yyyyyyep."

"The heads of the Gorgons should be disconnected from their bodies," Bacchus said, dropping the mime act. "And one should even be in this room, on your shield,

Minerva, if the screenplay is accurate. Legend says that Perseus presented Medusa's bagged head to you in thanks and that you mounted it to the front of your shield as a final defense in battle." Bacchus leaned Tamara's way, raised his hand beside his mouth, and stage-whispered, "Seems like cheating to me."

"You dare!" Minerva seethed.

"Aw, hell," Mars said. "Let's cut the crap. Minerva, rip the lambskin off that shield of yours and let's have a look, see if Medusa's head is really there or not."

"Well, that would actually kill us if it were there," Apollo said.

"But no king would receive an advisor into his chambers with a weapon that could wipe out his court." Everyone turned to see who spoke. I couldn't believe Tamara found her voice at such a precarious moment. "Would you, Your Highness?"

All eyes shot to Jupiter, whose gaze returned to Minerva.

"And Minerva couldn't risk carrying it around like that anyway," Tamara added, "here or anywhere, really. Suppose the lambskin slipped off the shield and someone important to her saw it? Suppose someone with designs for power made off with it."

"Hold your wagging tongue, peasant," Minerva hissed, "or I'll transform it into the snake it appears to be."

Tamara said no more, but no more words were

needed. Heads around the circle tilted in thought, and all eyes turned to Minerva. She reached for her shield, grabbed it by a twisted spike at its top edge, and pulled it to chest height. She looked around and threaded her left arm through the strap. The other hand she placed on the lambskin.

"Are you planning to expose us all to seeing a Gorgon?" Cupid asked. He looked back at his fiancé. "I think Tamara's right. Either you're storing that head else-where or you never got it in the first place. And if you never got it, what really happened to Medusa? You know what? I think you're bluffing. I don't think Medusa's head *is* on that shield."

"Don't you?" Minerva said, taking firm grip of the concealing hide.

"Nope. And I'm so sure it's not, I'll bet my life on it."

Chapter 12

A SLIPPERY TAIL

Cupid walked to where the dead vipers lay, behind Minerva. He pulled his arrow from the turquoise snake and set the dart to his bow.

"Strike a pose," Bacchus advised. "If you're to die, at least succumb in the most beautiful, dramatic way. I can hardly imagine more poetry and poignancy than to perish frozen in stone for eternity."

Cupid rolled his eyes so high it was almost out loud, but I noticed that he did position himself well before speaking.

"Okay, I'm all alone over here, Minerva. Let's see that head."

If she doesn't kill him now – with or without Medusa's head – she'll kill him later, Tamara thought.

Minerva didn't move. Every eye was trained on her.

"Would you like me to isolate them?" Apollo offered, already gathering some light.

"No need," Jupiter said, nodding at his son before looking to his daughter. "Remove the covering, Minerva."

Bacchus immediately struck a ridiculous pose with one leg back, another on tiptoe, one arm up, and the other trailing behind. Perhaps he wanted to be remembered as dancing through fields of flowers. No one else prepared themselves for an eternity of being gawked at as statues.

Minerva stalled. I could have listened in on her neebo. I'm sure I would have heard conflict. On one hand, she is the goddess of strategy in war and thus would tend to be more thoughtful with her actions than she exhibited today. On another hand, war is a part of her being. Violence was the basis of her childhood. And taunting dares can trigger unexpected behavior. I'd learned eons ago to not abuse my access into people's minds. It is a person's actions that define them more than the breadth of their thoughts. But Minerva had to comply with our king's demand, regardless of what her emotions or intellect said.

Her owl flapped its way to the edge of her shield. I sensed its allegiance. Minerva nodded her thanks before peeling the lambskin away from her gristled shield. Attached to its center by tendons and ligaments was a grotesque copper relief, oxidized to portray a hideous green face. A terrible reptilian countenance with snakes as hair. Wide, furious orbs for eyes. A protruding, forked tongue below surely venomous fangs.

But not a head of flesh and bone.

Bacchus dropped his pose along with his wide-eyed optimism. He wouldn't be eternally admired as a work of art. Better luck next time.

Fraud, Cupid thought. *Poser. Liar.* Instead of calling Minerva any of these names, he asked her, "Why the deception?"

"Because the reward suits me," Minerva answered.

"Of course," Tamara whispered.

"Speak up, my dear," Bacchus said. "We want to hear your conclusions."

Tamara shrunk a bit at the attention, but, because a god had demanded she speak, she straightened herself to do so. Cupid took to wing.

"However the legend started – and maybe Minerva started it herself – " Tamara began, "the reward was too great to set the record straight. Imagine the talk. 'Minerva has a deadly weapon.' Why would she dispute that? The fear brought on by such a weapon would freeze her enemies as surely as the weapon itself."

Cupid trained his arrow on Minerva. I knew he could control the function of his arrows to elicit love or just cause injury. This was the latter. I drew my bow and followed his lead. Mars grabbed an ax, probably to join whatever melee ensued, regardless of allegiances. Venus tossed a gauzy handkerchief off her dais for attention. She spoke.

"To seek advantage, all aspire.
To garner power, most admire.
Dishonored? Shunned? Her plans backfire!
She doth perspire, set in crossfire."

"Venus, I'll—" Minerva began.

"Thou and what army?" Venus sang.

Minerva dropped the lambskin and balled her

hand into a fist. I doubted she'd been this challenged in millennia.

"Now that everyone knows, Minerva, tell them where Medusa's head is," Jupiter demanded.

Minerva lowered the shield and bowed her head slightly. "On Medusa's neck. She lives."

"She lives!" crowed Bacchus, raising both arms. He circled the room waving them like they were stalks of wheat in a windstorm.

In the ERP, the Primordial continued its demolishing traipse on Earth.

Minerva ignored them both. "Perseus, that bleeding heart – uh, I mean, that sensitive demigod, your son," – she bowed her head lower to Jupiter – "pitied Medusa the moment he saw her reflection. Instead of liberating her vile head from her body, he told her why he was there, explained his foolish oath to acquire her head for his mother's oppressor, and begged her for help. Medusa circled him once, he said, and he lowered his shield and his eyes to make himself vulnerable. His cowering must have appealed to her vanity. She said something about always helping a woman against a controlling man and how teaming up with Perseus would not only help his mother but ultimately defy me. So she gave him a snake from her head. That cursed serpent was enough to destroy the mortal king. As an added benefit, it also killed a giant squid Neptune set around the island of Seriphos, so there's

Medusa's revenge on Neptune as well. Perseus even landed himself a princess bride from the island, so he ended up Medusa's number one fan."

Venus laughed, bells never tinkling so sweetly, before speaking.

> "And so thine assassin,
> his fierce weapons fastened
> firmly against his strong frame,
> discovered compassion,
> a friend, in a fashion,
> sparing the head thou wouldst claim."

"Ha HAAAA!" Bacchus shouted, bowing low to Venus.

Cupid veered toward Juno and fired an arrow over her shoulder. It impaled a grey, orange-banded kingsnake creeping up the council wall behind Bacchus. I heard its silent cry of pain in my mind and mourned it. It was a constrictor. It would have squeezed the life out of its victim, but that was its way, its natural majesty.

"What did you do to trigger Medusa?" Cupid asked Minerva, while Bacchus walked to the wall and claimed the trophy.

"Trigger her?" Minerva said, straightening to full height. "I've done nothing but forget her. I suppose the crazy girl can't deal with that."

"Oh, but, Minerva, an antagonist needn't be crazy," Bacchus said, waving the kingsnake's limp form as if wagging a finger at a naughty child. "Revenge as a motive is dangerous enough."

Chapter 13

THE MAGGOTS MOVE

W hat's dangerous is offending me not once but twice," Minerva said, beating a fist against her chest.

"Yes, well," Juno said. "Surely, you'll double curse her or whatever, but in the meantime we can't stay within these chambers." Juno allowed her dais to drift back to its spot beside the king. "The entire world is in danger, mortal and immortal. Jupiter, we cannot protect our subjects from inside."

"Finally!" Mars interjected. "We go to war."

"We are not all warriors with shiny shields," Bacchus said, placing a hand upon his heart. "I'm a lover, not a fighter."

"Would you *love* to be called a coward?" Mars asked.

Bacchus planted his index finger on his chin and thought a moment. "Shakespeare said, 'Cowards die many times before their deaths; the valiant never taste of death but once.' So from a certain point of view, I can handle death better than you."

Mars rolled the ax in his hand. "Oxygen thief."

Apollo dropped from his dais, which shrunk down to its former white disc and retracted into the wall from whence it came, signaling its owner's exit. "My horses will draw the sun of day in mere hours."

Mars grabbed a shield with his free hand. "Then let's roll, maggots. Darkness makes for a more dramatic theater."

"Theatre!" Bacchus cheered.

"Maggots?" Juno repeated, affronted.

Mars turned to Bacchus first. "You know I mean 'theater of war.' Put yer feathers away." Then to Juno, "I meant the royal court, Your Highness. It's a compliment."

She balked, but Mars pretended not to notice.

"We fight now," he commanded, "when the darkness hides everything, even the face of a Gorgon. If we catch a glimpse of that broad's mug in daylight, we'll all finish tits up."

Tamara shot Cupid an irritated glare.

I remember a time you looked at my dad with stars in your eyes, Cupid thought to himself, replaying their encounter at the Safe House on Earth. *You almost went away with him, but who's got you now?* He suppressed a grin and said to his father, "Commander."

"Mars is not a commander," Minerva corrected. "Because commanding requires strategic engagement. Mars only knows how to go balls to the wall."

Tamara sighed.

"Military slang war!" Bacchus said. "Oohrah!"

"Sir," Cupid continued. He twirled his hands and presented a watery block from which he stretched a strap. "Goggles made of turbulent water. The churning water will let you see shapes, but those shapes will be obscure. If the shape you see is long and skinny, Dad, it'll be a snake. Swing your ax. If it's our size or bigger and has only one fat leg, that leg is actually a tail, and the thing's a Gorgon. Swing."

Cupid tossed a pair of goggles to everyone.

"All right," Mars sang, snapping on his goggles. "Ladies, pull the back of your skirt forward and tuck it into your belt because we need to see legs! Here we go!" And, before anyone could argue the lunacy of going into battle half blind at night without any prep, Mars kicked out the council door and hurtled himself toward the first floor.

Jupiter leapt to his feet. He drove his staff into his dais to bring down the electric field.

Then everyone looked at each other wide-eyed before grabbing weapons and rushing after Mars. The maniac was likely to beat down the door and let any scaly thing slink its way in.

Chapter 14

CRUSH

Whoa!" Cupid exclaimed. We walked out of Council Colossus to find an alien land. Even through our cold, blurry goggles, in the darkest hour before dawn, we could see that the plaza was crawling with snakes. Their polished scales reflected the starlight above. They coiled and tangled. Every inch of Olympus slithered with serpentine bodies of every width, length, and color.

And the sound. Their scales scraped against each other like shells rolling in surf. Their hushed hiss was but a threatening kiss.

I was transported by the beauty before me, the simplicity of such agile creatures. Their musculature. Their shiny, elegant lengths. How I wished they weren't here. So many would die in an instant. The slinky mass twitched collectively as if they'd heard me, but no. They'd reacted to the electrical charge of Jupiter triggering his force field to protect the building behind us.

"Charge!" Mars yelled from ahead, and Cupid's neebo scrambled. I left my body right there, a few steps away from the doors of the CC, to transport myself to Cupid's mind to see as he did.

He unthinkingly obeyed. Cupid tore ahead, pulled an arrow from his quiver, and looked down the length of his arm to his bow's sight. He let loose an arrow on a black-, red-, and yellow-banded coral snake. The dart split it down the middle. It writhed and flopped in spasms as Cupid took to wing. His feet barely skimmed the rush.

Arrows discharged all around us as snakes encroached. Out of the corner of Cupid's eye, we saw Apollo shoot barb after barb. Minerva swung her sword. Cupid grabbed six arrows at once from his quiver and fired. No matter where his projectiles landed, they hit and killed snakes, whose bodies were overrun by more snakes advancing.

Mars plunged ahead on foot, happy to crush the enemy beneath his heel, heedless of the risk of vipers' fangs and Celestials' arrows. I suppose he thought himself impervious to both. Maybe he was.

Cupid kept firing. I sensed no anger, just defense.

He looked back at Juno. The queen pointed into the surge. Her peacock lowered his head and ran. When the royal bird reached a whorl of snakes, he flapped for lift and tore in with his razor-sharp talons. His huge tail balanced him. Fangs struck. Rope-bodies ensnared. Screeching. Hissing.

That bird's done for, Cupid thought.

He looked around and spotted Bacchus pointing to the statuary above. He beckoned with his index finger, and marble vines cracked free of their lithic homes to whip into the surge.

Niiiiiice move, Cupid thought.

I never imagined that rock-ribbed vines could move as lithely as reptiles, but the snakes were outdone. The vines soon choked them and freed the peacock to fight anew.

Cupid looked past Jupiter, who wasn't lifting a finger to help, to check on Tamara. We were both surprised to discover her surveying my inert form near the main doors. My body stood static while my consciousness hovered in Cupid's mind. Tamara circled my body, shield in hand, intrigued.

She caught us looking – well, Cupid, looking. "What's wrong with her?" Tamara asked. "I can't tell through these goggles."

I could have abandoned Cupid and returned to myself, but there was hardly any point. I was not going to fight the snakes, and the goggles protected me well enough.

"Diana's ... dazed, I think," Cupid shouted back. "Oh gods, is she ... seeing a prophecy or something?"

"Maybe," Tamara called back, waving a hand before my eyes.

"Well, stay with her in case she chants an incantation or something," Cupid said. "Whoa!"

We felt a sting. Cupid scraped his cheek and came away with scales and hide. He looked past his hand to see snakes flying our way. Not whole snakes. Mars was swinging through them, sweeping his ax from side to side and hacking swaths of them to bits.

"They're swarming!" Tamara called.

Cupid looked to see a wave rushing Minerva. The onslaught was brown and black and leathery.

"Off, vermin!" Minerva shouted at the dozen snakes that came up from behind to sink their fangs into the gristle armor at her elbow. She dislocated them with a snap, but more snakes lurched her way. She rebuffed with her shield. They cracked their heads and dropped unconscious onto the flood of serpents at her feet. The oncoming wave crested, swept across, and inundate her.

It was a beautiful attack.

"Swim up," Cupid shouted, snapping me out of my reverie. He fired so many arrows into the flow that I wondered whether Minerva would survive to escape. But Cupid thinned the top of the deluge, and Minerva's sword broke through.

"Pin her, my friendsssssssss," came a raspy voice from the center of the plaza. Cupid looked over, and we saw a blurry figure slide out from behind Janus. Its green "leg" was surely too thick to be anything but a tail. The figure's torso was feminine, and its head…oh, its head! Thin forms swayed around it, rising on end and dipping low. Living hair. Snakes. I was sure it was the same Gorgon we'd seen earlier behind the water wall.

"Gorgo-o-o-o-o-o-o-n!" Mars shouted. He pivoted and charged her way.

She pointed with her bow. At her command, hundreds of snakes leapt out of the swarm at his feet to bind his wrists. Others sunk their fangs into their brethren, creating a bleeding but powerful rope that tethered him to a hundred snakes and more. They bound his ankles and wrapped themselves around his neck before Cupid began firing faster than a machine gun.

"Minerva!" Apollo shouted. Cupid looked over long enough to see constrictors set upon her neck and wrap her head like a mummy. Pythons pulled her under the swell. Apollo fired white-hot laser beams off his fingertips. He'd hit Minerva, too, I had no doubt.

A shout pierced the chaos.

We followed it to find Juno lunging toward her peacock, which had turned to stone midair. It was raised in attack. Its long tail feathers tethered it to the ground, perfectly balanced. It would have made an artisan masterpiece had it not been real moments before.

A scream, and we turned to find its source near the CC doors.

Cupid's heart plummeted when he saw Tamara ripping garter snakes away from her face. These weren't the powerful snakes attacking the gods. These were babies, small as drinking straws, tiny enough to be swimming within her goggles. The more joined in, the faster they pulled her goggles apart. Tamara flung them away as fast as she could, but they were breaking the water's cohesion.

The goggles would fall apart.

Cupid thrust both hands toward his father. Water burst forth as if out of a water cannon. The snakes disengaged and were thrown. Cupid didn't wait to see where Mars landed. He turned back to Tamara and threw water at her. The globs slapped onto her face and clung to her goggles. But bigger snakes joined their tiny twins. They separated the water. Within seconds, the snakes fell from Tamara's face altogether. There was no more water to hold them up.

Tamara looked at Cupid wide-eyed before turning around to see me, still inert, with snakes swarming my goggles. She tried to pull them away, but they too broke the water's stability. Tamara clamped a hand over my open eyes and leaned in.

It was at that moment that Cupid and I saw a large figure rise behind my motionless body. It was grey and mottled. Its hair waved. The figure grew taller as it hoisted itself on its tail. It lifted a hand gloved in brass as if to strike.

Tamara froze in place.

It took a moment before Cupid and I understood that she wasn't standing still to avoid detection.

I felt Cupid's heart rip into a million pieces as we realized together that Tamara had been turned to stone.

Chapter 15

OVERRUN

"Noooooo!" Cupid wailed and lunged toward Tamara. I had only begun to register his fury when I was thrown back into my body and toppled by a blast of sleet.

Hail pelted me and battered every surface. It shorted Jupiter's electric field before bringing it down altogether. Updrafts of rain from every direction picked up a thousand snakes and sent them hurtling. Only the Gorgons had the mass and strength to keep their ground. Their hefty scales gripped the cloud deck like a vice, and they side-winded, disappearing into the sudden fog.

"Come back and fix her, you witches!" Cupid bellowed midair, but he didn't pursue. He landed behind Tamara, ripped off his goggles, and put both hands on her shoulders. "Tamara. TamTam," he called, shuffling around her, touching her arm, her hair, her face. Once he stood before her, in the place I'd been, he spoke more softly. "Tam Baby? Tam?"

Her expression barely showed fright. Someone who didn't know her might not register that her eyes were a bit wider than normal and her mouth just barely open. Her right hand was cemented high, palm out, and I knew why. In her final moment, she'd tried to block my eyes from seeing. Her left arm embraced the space my shoulder had been. She'd tried to keep me close.

Cupid's expression said heart-wrenchingly more. His eyes twitched side to side, searching hers. His jaw quivered.

"Tamara, Honey." His breath came out short. He brought his hands to the side of her face and tapped her cheeks. "Come on, Peach. Talk to me."

She didn't speak. She didn't move.

Cupid lowered his hands and patted her shoulders. "Come on, Princess." His breath hitched. "Please, please talk to me. Please move."

Nothing moved.

I couldn't breathe.

Cupid wrapped his arms around her and whispered into her ear, "Ma chérie." He drew back just enough to turn in and kiss her unmoving lips. "My love." He brushed his cheek against hers. "My dove," he murmured. "Please, kiss me back."

A tear ran down my cheek. Cupid's face was awash in them.

"Tamara, come back to me, Baby." His voice broke. "G-give me a sign."

She didn't respond.

My knees felt wobbly.

Cupid embraced her cold, unyielding body.

"You … you can't be …" And then Cupid collapsed

at her stone feet. His entire world fell away. His neebo screamed in agony.

I toppled over. I'd never felt life extinguish through heartache, but more than half of Cupid's neebo died in the instant. The rest suffered horribly in loss, anguish, and hopelessness. I telepathized the neebo through my pain to save themselves, to flee, but not one left him. Only the strongest had survived the grief at all. Their bond to him would be fierce. They'd stay with him forever.

"Come back to me, Sweetheart," Cupid moaned. "I can't ..."

The freezing water that swept through Olympus moments ago cascaded down in a cold, bitter rain that soaked Cupid's curved back and drooped wings. Tears dripped off the end of Cupid's nose to land on Tamara's stone toes. I felt my chest ripping. His emotions were too powerful this close. I stepped away to sob alone.

Time passed, who knows how much, before the other gods returned. Perhaps they'd too been thrown. Or maybe they went in pursuit of the Gorgons and their mob while it was still dark. Everything felt shadowed and unreal. We heard shuffling, then gasps.

"No," Bacchus said, hushed. "No. Not Tamara."

Cupid's sobs were joined by another's.

I looked up to see Venus crying into the upswept cloth of her gown. She raised her tearful face from her hands and sputtered,

"What kindness lost!
Within, without,
a heart of love
now oh! snuffed out.
Our hero, she!
A guiding light.
Her final deed
a sacrifice!
My son, undone,
his love so true.
My heart doth bleed,
'Tis rent in two."

She sobbed. The rest of us stood around Cupid and Tamara, he at her feet, broken and weeping, for what seemed like ages. Only Mars turned away, either to fend off witnessing his son's distress or to keep watch as the only one still wearing goggles.

Parchment notes began materializing all around us. They went ignored as we bore witness to Cupid's anguish.

"I can't … accept this," Cupid said, looking up. "We're supposed to be immortal. Jupiter, why isn't Tamara immortal?"

"Immortality is relative," Jupiter said. "To mortals,

we do indeed live forever. We don't die of old age, and we regenerate quickly. But we can be killed, Cupid, by those as powerful as ourselves."

"The Gorgons were mortals!" Cupid shouted. "How can they be as powerful as us?!"

"Minerva made them so," I answered, no small hint of anger in my tight voice.

She shot me a hateful look, but there was no denying her role in this.

Cupid got to his feet. Rain sloshed off his wings. His swollen eyes held an ocean of tears. "Isn't there anything we can do to save her?"

Bacchus dug his hands into his oversized pockets and pulled out five or six bite-sized squares of ambrosia. He rushed over and rubbed them on Tamara's arm. I saw a scene in his mind of an ambrosia bath healing Cupid from the poisoning of a manchineel tree. The ambrosia did nothing for Tamara. Bacchus hung his head.

Jupiter stepped forward. "The Gorgons have taken hundreds, if not thousands, of lives since they were turned—"

"The lives of those who sought to kill them," I interrupted.

"Regardless," Jupiter went on. "Bacchus, we've tried ambrosia before. It doesn't help the gorgonized."

"We need to try more," Cupid said with desperation in his voice. He held out a hand. From the fog zoomed his silver ambrosia tray. Cupid snagged it midair and waved a hand above it. Nothing. He looked at Jupiter.

"Perhaps the chefs are in hiding," Jupiter offered, but his wavering eyes belied his calm voice.

"There has to be some way to save Tamara," Cupid insisted. "There has to be. Apollo, you're the god of healing. Is there anything that can be done? Please say yes. Please."

Apollo placed a hand on each side of his head. I'd seen Apollo think deeply this way only a few times in our entire existence. The dark plaza seemed to get darker, but maybe that was because all eyes were on him. Cupid held his breath for the answer, and I found myself doing the same.

"There is one possibility, Cupid, but it's uncertain and danger—"

"I'll do it," Cupid insisted. "Whatever it is, I'll do it. Whatever it takes."

"Cupid," Apollo said, stepping forward and arresting him with a hand to the shoulder. "Anti-venom can sometimes arrest the damage from a venom strike. Tamara wasn't bitten, but perhaps the premise is the same. Perhaps the answer lies within the Gorgons themselves, maybe in their eyes or their blood or their venom that turns those who gaze upon them into stone. But, Cupid, testing this theory could cost you your life."

"Being without Tamara has already cost me my life."

Apollo sighed. "I cannot guarantee results. You'd

have to get ahold of them—"

"By any means necessary," Cupid finished.

"Yes!" Mars called over his shoulder. "War!"

"You don't have to kill them," I insisted to Cupid.

"Why are you still defending the Gorgons?!" he barked, turning to me with rage in his eyes. He pointed to Tamara. "Don't you see her?"

"The Gorgons never before sought anything but to be left alone," I said steadily. "Unlike the Primordials, they never sought chaos. There's a reason why they're here."

"Pluto will be dealt with for his failure to contain the Primordials," Jupiter answered, completely missing my point.

"*I'll* bring you the Gorgons' heads, Apollo," Minerva offered, "and all the venom each holds."

Cupid turned on her with bared teeth and fisted hands. "You'll take Tamara inside and you'll guard her with your life." The cold rain slammed down in a deluge, stinging like knives. Cupid stuck a finger in Minerva's face. "The snakes went after *you*, Minerva. *You're* the reason they're here. If Tamara's body is damaged in your care or if she can't be saved later, I'll finish what the Gorgons started with you, and I'll keep it up for all of eternity."

Over Cupid's shoulder, Mars turned and ripped off his goggles. He glared at Minerva in a show of solidarity. Venus stepped to Cupid's side.

Minerva stood her ground but switched her blade

from one hand to the other, perhaps reminding everyone, if it came to it, that she was armed.

Cupid turned toward his father. "Dad, I need a sword."

A scimitar was in Cupid's hand almost before he finished the sentence.

"Good for slashing," Mars explained. "They don't get stuck in flesh like a straight sword."

"And I need your shield," Cupid demanded of Minerva.

She balked. "Never."

"Yield your shield," Jupiter said. "You have others inside."

Minerva looked away in anger. "Allow me to retrieve the lambskin."

"Your reputation means nothing compared to my fiancée," Cupid said. He stepped forward and snatched her shield. She balled her fist but could do nothing in the face of Jupiter's demand.

Cupid tossed the shield into the air and set a rolling water bubble under it so the shield spun on its edge, its inside toward us. Cupid then tossed a glob of water against it, which spread to the edge and clung like a fine coating. "Your Highness, would you please add dust and heat?"

Jupiter nodded with a knowing smile. He pulled stardust out of his robes and tossed it into the water coating. He then gathered a thunderbolt, forcing the rest of us to step back. When he hurled the bolt onto the shield, the weapon burst into flame. It continued rolling, refining the stardust. When the fire dissipated, the shield's back shone bright with a polish unmatched by even the finest silver-backed mirror.

Cupid threaded his arm through the shield's enarme and promised, "I'll bring back Medusa dead or alive."

"We'll fight together, Son," Mars said, but Cupid shot him down.

"The council needs your protection, as does Tamara."

"I'll go with you," Bacchus offered. "I wouldn't miss this for all the worlds."

"As shall I," I said.

"I don't need you interfering," Cupid warned.

I bristled at the wrongheadedness but nodded toward Apollo and said, "We twins do well when covering multiple camps. And 'twas I who brought you here."

Cupid didn't reply. His remaining neebo were furious with me.

"I'll force an early dawn," Apollo said. "It will terrify the mortals, but the sun will chase away the cover of darkness and light your way."

He raised his hands. We heard an echoing series of whinnies off to the east. A few moments later, his horses pulled his chariot and the sun not only over Earth's horizon but over our own, high above Earth.

Apollo's horses had eons of practice pulling the sun behind them, but today they looked exuberant. Their mouths frothed and their muscles pulsed as they yanked their charge in its fastest ascent ever. They didn't know the reason for it, just the joy of the unprecedented sprint. Their gallop turned darkness into full daylight in a matter of seconds. If mortals were still paying attention to weather after news of the Primordial, this unnatural daybreak would add to their panic.

The sudden sunshine burned away the fog and revealed the magnitude of the Gorgons' forces. Council Colossus was littered with shed snakeskins. In some spots, a passerby would wade in up to her knees. And though we were far from Olympus' city center, we could see the skyline crawling. Putrid smoke rose all around. Jupiter Heights, normally glowing white, looked dirty brown, overrun with snakes.

"That's where we start," Cupid said and added to Minerva, "Protect her with your very life." He took off without us.

Bacchus and I looked at each other.

"I can't fly without assistance," I said.

"Me either. I'll call my panthers."

"I've got better," Mars said. He turned and bellowed, "Wolves!" An instant later, a pack of enormous wolves charged over a distant hill heading our direction. The creatures were made entirely of gold. Their withers rippled as they ran and glinted in the sun's rays.

Mars held up two fingers. The majority of the pack slid to a halt and turned back. Two kept coming. Mars pointed at us. The charging canines bared their fangs in acknowledgment. "They're war wolves, from the reliefs of my chariot. And being made of gold, they can't be turned to stone. Let Medusa choke on that." Mars chuckled. The stampeding wolves didn't even alter their rhythm as they left the cloud deck and ran on air.

Mars nodded at us. "Better get ready to jump on. They won't stop."

"What?!" Bacchus shouted.

"Pretend you're a rodeo clown mutton busting. You can be a clown, can't you, Bacchus?" Mars grinned.

"But that's no sheep I'd be riding!" Bacchus argued with seconds to go before the wolves were upon us.

"Surely you've hopped on your panthers," I called, readying myself to jump astride my ride, pleased once again about my choice of short leather skirt rather than long godly robe. "Here we go!"

I took a running start, swung a leg, and landed perfectly. Bacchus dove above the wolf's path and belly-flopped onto its back. Mars' booming laughter chased us, but we were on our way, with Cupid in our sights.

Chapter 16

ENTRY

Cupid slowed to hover above Ceres Plaza. When we caught up, Bacchus righted himself, and we too saw what arrested Cupid. The bamboo water fountain at center plaza was encircled in sloughed snakeskin a foot deep. The fountain itself wasn't stopped up by skins but rather lassoed by them.

We were high up, and we instinctively took a glance around Olympus. Most other celestial water fountains were fully clogged. The whitish, papery membrane of snakeskin floated in the still water or hung off the statue's outcroppings, here snagged on a jagged crown, there pulled off by a sharp bronze bow.

"That's weird," Cupid muttered, his eyes settling again on the Ceres Fountain. "The snakes didn't shed in this fountain."

"Is it weird, Cupid, really?" I answered.

Cupid frowned. *Ceres is the goddess of grain,* he thought, picturing a vast field of golden, waving grain. "Her fields."

"Yes, Cupid," I said. "Ceres' fields provide snakes a peaceful home with shelter and all the scurrying rodents they can eat. Her domain makes their very existence possible, and their allegiance to her would be strong. Along with allegiance to Medusa."

Cupid's eyes flashed.

"Cupid," I said, "your rage and sadness are justified, but to triumph you must step outside yourself and see others' points of view."

"Like Tamara's point of view?" Cupid barked. "Or like all the other lives those Gorgon vermin have extinguished?"

"Cupid," Bacchus said, stepping in before the conversation turned ugly. "Think of this as theatre."

"You think of everything as theater," Cupid spat.

"True," Bacchus acknowledged with a nod, "because it's so very useful. Look around. This story narrative is new. Think back to the previous chapters in your personal saga. Pluto and Mercury as antagonists went after you, their antihero, to eliminate an obstacle and snag the reigns of power, a tried and true plot line sure to please an audience."

"What audience?!" – *you nutjob,* Cupid added in his head.

"All the world's a stage," Bacchus answered, "but never mind that. Haven't you noticed the twist of plot here? Medusa went after Minerva, not you. And the Gorgon who petrified Tamara stood behind Diana. It was *Tamara* who turned to see *her.* If the Gorgon had wanted to turn her to stone, she'd have risen earlier and on the other side, closer to you, as a matter of fact."

Cupid's face was expressionless, but his neebo were

a jangle.

"The winningest heroes of all classic tales heed the premonitions of seers," Bacchus advised.

"Seers have brought me nothing but grief," Cupid replied.

"Cupid," I said. "Think. If the snakes are obeying Medusa now, why might they still respect Ceres' fountain?"

Cupid frowned again and grudgingly searched his memory. I urged his neebo to linger on the specifics. *Jupiter built this fountain to apologize to Ceres for not moving fast enough to save her daughter.*

He remembered the myth, a true story in this case. Ceres and her daughter Proserpina were collecting flowers, minding their own business, as we gods in the ecological arts tend to do, when Pluto burst through a cleft in the earth and nabbed the daughter. He dragged Proserpina to The Underworld, where naturally her mother couldn't see her. Ceres searched so long, she neglected her work, and the Earth's harvests failed. Some even say Ceres forbade the earth from producing to force other gods to help her search. Either way, Jupiter heard the cries of starving mortals and forced Pluto to release the girl. Unfortunately, Proserpina had eaten in The Underworld – pomegranate seeds, of all things – so she was bound to return half of every year. Ever since, Ceres mourns her daughter's forced return to her abductor, triggering fall and winter. When Proserpina and Ceres reunite, Earth bursts forth the vegetation of spring and summer.

Jupiter thought a fountain was a good way to commemorate his intervention and bizarre compromise.

"Jarel!" Cupid said. I looked up to see the final member of the Fallen Four, the one who missed Cupid's proposal to Tamara. This angel's brown, friendly face seemed trim for his otherwise fleshy body. I was surprised that his small wings could carry him all the way to Olympus, especially loaded down as he was with studded leather armor, an enormous metal kite shield, and at least a half dozen swords hanging from his wide, branded belt. I couldn't understand how his pants stayed up.

"Cupid, I come soon's I could see day," Jarel said, panting. "Cool wolves," he said to Bacchus and me. He turned back to Cupid. "Wus happening?"

Cupid turned on the spot and dropped his head into his hands. I felt another wave of anguish.

"Cupid! Sup?!"

Bacchus quickly relayed the tragic news. Jarel immediately wailed, his cry echoing across the plaza. Bacchus' neebo told me he'd met Jarel before, so it was no surprise when he placed a consoling hand on Jarel's head and advised him to help us or go to the CC to guard Tamara.

"But I was jes' at the CC, and dey din't say nuttin,'" he said. "When I came up on 'em, only Mars, Venus, and Jupiter was still outside. Da others must'a gone in. Mars asked wha' I been doin,' and I says helpin' Vulcan fight da Primordial cuz Mars shore wadn't helpin' no one. And I pointed out to Mars dat he be spendin' more'n half his time with Venus, so ain't no point bein' his apprentice cuz I ain't been learnin' no fightin.' An' I tell Mars he more a love god than he wanna admit, and Mars got real mad at dat, and he pulled a knife an' everythin' but den Miss Venus shifted her weight or flicked her hair or some'n as simple as dat, and Mars notices and fergets all 'bout my quittin' him and he goes in afta her, jes provin' my point, and Jupiter tells me ta go after yous three, so here I am."

"Good," Bacchus says. "We need you. You sound different, you know."

"I don't say 'yuh' no mo'. Mars smacked me e'ry time I did. Said it was a 'noying quirk and drove him nuts, so I got smacked until I stopped sayin' it. 'Sa crappy way to teach some'n, but I reckon it worked. Makes me wonder 'bout Cupid's child'ood."

A flood of scenes flashed through Cupid's mind of his father dragging him to battle scenes and picking fights with complete strangers and berating love every chance he got. It impressed me that a child so diminished could become so powerful.

That's when I heard it.

Wha- what happened?

It couldn't be, but there it was.

Why am I – I can't talk. I can't move! Why can't I

move?!

It was Tamara. Her thoughts. Her neebo.

Still with us.

Alive.

Help! she screamed. *Help! Cupid!*

"We can still save Tamara," I blurted – without thought about how to do so or how my words might haunt Cupid if we failed.

"I'm counting on it. But we can't if we stay here," Cupid said. "Jarel, Bacchus can show you how to use that shield against Medusa."

"I know how ta use a shield!" Jarel protested.

"No, Cupid. You don't understand. I-" I stopped myself. If I revealed that I could hear Tamara, it wouldn't be long before everyone deduced that maybe I could hear their thoughts too. I saved the neebo long ago at least in part to understand people's reactions to the present. Without the neebo, I'd be imprisoned in the future, looking through my oracle eye to see what *might* happen. That 'not knowing what the current day brings' nonsense is fine for a mortal, but not for a goddess.

"Cupid, I-I sense biological essence within her," I clarified.

"She was just transformed, Diana," Bacchus said. "Isn't it natural that you should sense lingering biotraces?"

"Not in stone. I sense life."

Cupid looked at me with unwavering eyes. "Then

we hurry. We take a Gorgon back to Apollo to try to heal Tamara."

He spun to face Jupiter Heights once more. Jarel fluttered beside him. Bacchus and I guided our wolves alongside. I considered with trepidation that it was just us six – because I had no doubt the wolves would do their part – going into a building so swarming with snakes that it looked like a living, breathing thing itself. The surface seemed to sway as countless slinks scurried up and down it. I wondered if it, like a giant tree burdened under the sheer weight of the living upon it, might fold. But the sight was beautiful in a creepy crawly kind of way.

Jarel handed Bacchus and me swords from the many on his belt, and we tucked them into our own belts before shooting toward the building. Time was of the essence.

As we got closer, the brown mass of snakes revealed a mix of every color imaginable, from turquoise blue to sunshine yellow. They pulled their heads away from the building wall upon which they clung. Thousands of forked tongues flicked our way, tasting our presence and no doubt alerting their mistresses that intruders were coming. I regretted feeling like one, but I was as solid in my purpose as Cupid. Regardless of any sympathies for the Gorgons' lot, we needed to take one back to the CC. Tamara needed saving.

Cupid calculated as we approached. *The snakes will*

strike. I can't clear our path with water – that only makes them more agile. And Diana won't convince them to make space.

I felt his dirty look but ignored it. We were fast approaching the castle's 20-foot-tall pearl doors. No snakes clung directly to them. The doors were likely too polished to provide purchase. But the legless tubers worked a way around that, as snakes so often do. A row of them hung above the door, their heads and tails clinging to the door-frame's marble, and their middles forming loops. A second row of snakes looped through the first and so on until the doors were curtained in chains of snakes. Only those anchoring the very top suffered. I watched them wriggle their scales over and over to re-grip the marble, to find the stone's pitting and rough fissures, to keep themselves aloft.

While the rest of the snake curtain didn't move much, I felt the vertical slits of a thousand other eyes flick our way. Other snakes were ready to pounce. The sound of so many scales skimming the building reminded me of ocean waves scraping beach sand. The hissing, though, was ominous.

How do we get past them? Cupid thought just as Bacchus called out, "Vines!" A second later, winding ten-drils hurtled from every direction toward the castle door.

"Flora!" I called. More vegetation flew forth, what-ever Celestials had planted in nearby gardens. Tall grasses and short shrubs and flowers extinct on Earth but thriving in heaven shot forward to join Bacchus' vines in front of the pearl door. They intertwined, spread out, and formed a tube, just ten meters long, making a barrier between serpents and Celestials. The tube wasn't hard like concrete. It was organic and porous and would only divide us from our attackers for a few seconds.

Snakes as long as the tube itself dropped from the building's heights and thudded onto it. They pushed their faces into the weaving but couldn't find gaps big enough to burrow into. Several encircled the tube and began squeezing. It compressed. They'd collapse our passageway.

"Hurry!" Cupid called.

We leaned into our charge.

What looked like rain pitter-pattered onto the tube. But I knew these dousing drops were snakes, the smallest of them. These three-inch threadsnakes, thin as worms, could burrow their way through vines and leaves. They could drop onto us and slide their bending bodies into our eyes and ears. Not even the neebo could prevent their devastation.

"Don't stop!" Cupid warned.

"Y'all is gods! Can't you fix this?" Jarel shouted.

"Just move!" Cupid ordered.

We soared into the tube. I looked back and saw the opening collapse behind us as an anaconda crushed it. A darkly spotted aquatic snake tumbled in through the break. I looked forward to see Cupid and Jarel ready to crash into the door.

"Now!" Bacchus yelled, and the vines forming the tunnel lunged with us. They rammed the door just as Cupid slammed his shoulder into it. The portal gave way, and Cupid rolled into the building. Jarel zipped in behind him. Bacchus, the wolves, and I barely outflew a second anaconda on our tails. Jarel kicked the door shut. Before it slammed home, we saw Bacchus' precious vines crushed under an avalanche of snakes.

We leapt to our feet and faced the door, waiting for the colubrine horde to batter its way in as we had. They thudded against the door just once, and then there was silence.

We stood still as statues.

C'mon, you belts-in-the-making, Cupid thought.

Nothing.

But wait. We did hear something. Music. Soft and mesmerizing. Bacchus and I looked back to see that we'd landed at the base of a grand, opal-iridescent double stairway leading into the clouds.

"Don't get lost in the stairs," Cupid warned, and Bacchus and I looked back to see Jarel and Cupid still at the ready. A hiss brought us all to our senses.

"Formation!" Cupid yelled, and we snapped into a circle, faces toward each other with raised shields. The stance was the absolutely wrong defense for normal combat. If we were a group of four surrounded by hostiles, the last thing we'd do is present the large and easy target of our backs, but we knew what awaited us here inside this house of horrors, and we knew the right move instinctively.

The reflections in our shields revealed softly glowing white walls that began to weep inky strips of color.

"No one's got ophidiophobia I hope, a fear of snakes?" I quipped.

"We can't escape them either way," Cupid said by way of answer and looked around. "There was no point in our closing the door. They're already inside."

Jarel shook his head as dozens of snakes slid down the walls, looking like dripping paint. "Don't think so, Cupid. Deys enough snakes in dese parts for dem to be all new snakes."

"Do you have any idea what that means?" Bacchus said, nodding into his shield. "Do you know how many snakes that portends?"

"Earth has more than three thousand species," I answered. "Olympus has a fair few, too. And each species has countless members. That's why they're so very successful."

Cupid looked back into his shield. *They're not looking at us,* Cupid thought to himself with curiosity. *They're not reacting to us at all.*

We watched as the snakes reached out to one another and intertwined themselves, not just vertically like they had outside, but horizontally, too, forming a sort of netting, like ants making a bridge of their bodies. Scores of snakes slid down the walls, latching onto others. Then scores more.

"They're coating the walls," Cupid said. "Why would they do that rather than attack?"

The hall quickly darkened as less and less of the castle's glowing white walls shone through.

Chapter 17

GOAT

"If we can't see walls," Jarel deduced out loud, "how we gonna know we following de walls at all?"

"We won't," Bacchus said with a nod that showed he was impressed. "The snakes will be able to maneuver us. They can make sure we get lost."

"Shields up!" Cupid demanded. "We'll find the Gorgons no matter what tricks they pull. Backwards march!"

"'S'a slow way ta advance," Jarel noted.

"We can't risk walking forward," Cupid replied with frustration. "Even if we raised our shields behind us and looked back over our shoulder, there'd be too much temptation to quickly look where we're headed."

"Just pretend you're a theatre critic," Bacchus said. "You're talentless, so you creep through life backward hoping your targets don't zero in."

We lined up for our reverse incursion. I watched through my shield's reflection as the wolves took the lead, walking forward without fear, their heads held high. Their golden bodies were impervious to two of the most infamous weapons in a Gorgonian arsenal: petrifaction and arrows. And, lacking flesh, they were safe from a neebo infestation. What was still a threat to them, though, was the Gorgons' third weapon of choice, the sledgehammer.

Our lupine companions swatted at a pair of copperheads swaying at eye level on the wall. The pit vipers bared their venomous fangs before shifting their section of wall, swinging it out from an imaginary hinge and changing the path.

Cupid stopped. "We can't let them steer us."

"Yeah, cuz dey'll take us ta where da Gorgons wants us to go, a place to dey advantage, or maybe nowheres near 'em."

"Such pageantry!" Bacchus said. "This beautifully dramatic scene, snakes forming catacombs that we heroes must penetrate at risk of life itself on our quest to save the kingdom!"

"You NUTCASE!" Cupid roared. "We're not saving the kingdom. We're saving Tamara. Remember her? The girl you wanted to steal so badly you trapped me in a lava tunnel so that I'd be burned to bits or eaten by your panthers?"

"Oh, that was beautiful too," Bacchus said, his eyes drifting off his shield. His neebo showed me the narrow escape from their earlier adventures.

Cupid's neebo emitted plain disgust as he turned to Jarel. "We either cut our way through them or we follow the path they make."

Jarel raised his sword behind him. Cupid nodded.

I watched in horror as Jarel cut his way through the

wall. He sliced serpents of every size clean through, and, as their limp, halved bodies dropped from the collective, Jarel stepped backward and past them. As soon as his shield breached the gash he'd made, a rush of fresh snakes closed the gap. Jarel disappeared from sight.

"No!" Cupid yelled, and leapt backward to the same spot. He was amazing with his scimitar. Much more elegant than Jarel. Cupid swept the sword in a huge arch behind him, creating a perfect hole, large enough for us to hop through, even the wolves. More snakes dropped from above, volunteering to lose their lives in defense of keeping us on path, but they were too late. We'd broken through their wall and found what they'd hoped to keep hidden.

A giant room spread before us with all the hanging pots and long tables that a royal kitchen demands. But this was no longer a kitchen. It was a statuary. A few dozen Celestials in *toques blanches* stood trapped in stone. Some wielded spoons in their final second, one held a rolling pin aloft, a few were bent low to reach into steel cabinetry, but all faced us, immobile. We stood where the Gorgons had when they turned the royal chefs to stone.

"No wonder your ambrosia tray yielded nothing," Bacchus said. "No one's getting ambrosia service."

Jarel shook his head.

"The hungry will live," Cupid said, "for a few days at least. The Gorgons are who we're after, and they're not here. We move on. Follow the path. But we need a way to make sure we aren't walking in circles."

I raised my shield. The nearest plant in the castle uprooted itself from its planter and flew onto the disk. I thanked it before demanding it dissect itself. Petals plucked themselves from their flowers. Leaves tore from their stems. They settled on the edge of my shield except for a few roots that stayed center. Those arranged themselves to depict the path we'd taken so far.

Cupid, please help.

Tamara's thoughts were breaking through to me again.

Can anyone hear me? I'm trapped.

I looked to Cupid only to find him staring at me.

"What do you see?" he asked.

"A need for urgency."

Cupid turned back the way we came. This time he had no need for his scimitar. The snakes separated to allow him back into the main hall. The wall of them shifted. At once, my organic tracker rearranged itself to show our new path and assure us that we wouldn't be set on a loop.

We walked until our arms quivered from holding shields aloft. And we walked more, until our calves ached from the labor of a backward gait. And still more, until our eyes strained in the low light. The smell, musky and stifling as a foul cave, suffocated us. Snakes soon coated the ground, so we walked atop them. I could feel their long spines and fragile ribs dip under our weight. I also sensed that we were rising ever so slightly, being taken up a level. Cupid kept peering over his shield to my navigation map. I, on the other hand, couldn't quite pay attention to it as Apollo was sharing his sight with me.

An endless supply of parchments was materializing in the CC and fluttering down to the main floor where the gods ignored them to deal with their own infestation.

I mentally leapt into Juno's head. She was employing her least used powers, those of memory and order. She waved her hand over every snake that approached her, and the serpentine soldier forgot why it was there. It turned and slunk away. But I felt Juno's deep breaths. The work was taxing, and the room was hot.

I leapt back into Apollo's mind to discern why the room was so stifling. I found him staring at Venus. His passion roared like fire, and my overwrought brother radiated heat.

The goddess of beauty and sexuality was dancing. Provocatively. Her chest and hips were draped in a shimmering scarf. Her hips rolled and swayed. She glowed under the red light emitted by Apollo, but she paid him no attention. She was luring snakes.

A smirking Mars ran through the mesmerized

snakes unthreatened, killing swaths of them with a single, running sweep of his sword.

The light on Venus changed from blood red to butter yellow. Apollo was growing hotter. I couldn't stand his thoughts, so I leapt back into Juno and inclined her neebo to look his way.

The snakes, cold-blooded bobbers that they are and drawn to Venus' charm as they were, nonetheless turned course toward my brother's enticing temperature. Mars turned, too, and bisected the lot heading toward my immodest brother. The grimace on Mars' face said all anyone needed to know. Once he'd swept over the snakes, he turned back to punch Apollo hard in the face.

Interestingly, Juno's eyes snapped away from Apollo, for whom she felt no concern, over to her husband, to check that he wasn't equally ogling Venus. But the king of the gods had wisely turned his back on the whole situation. He was zapping snakes at his feet with the tip of a thunderbolt .

"Stop it!"

Juno looked back to see Minerva stomp toward Mars and jab a spear tip to his throat.

"Divided forces succumb to their attacker! Apollo is not the enemy here!"

Minerva looked around the room. Juno did the same and saw the gravity of their situation. Snakes continued to approach from all sides. They slithered under doors, crept around walls, and pushed through the tiniest of ventilation slits. Even with all six gods present and fighting, they were being distracted from the real fight, the one with the Gorgons, and they risked being overrun.

"Your highness," Minerva said, directing her words to Jupiter, "The ground floor is overrun. I recommend we retreat to council chambers."

The thunder god hurtled the bolt in his hand at Tamara. It lifted her petrified form and shot her toward the top floor.

I was glad for a moment that Cupid couldn't see this vision with me. Stone is a terrible conductor of electricity, so Tamara wouldn't be hurt. Still, there was a certain brutality to seeing a loved one struck by lightning.

The gods followed Tamara, dragging me along. As soon as we entered chambers, we saw Pluto's face so large within Jupiter's ERP that anyone would have sworn he was pressed against the glass, if it existed. Pluto's hand was wrapped around a human's throat. He chuckled when he saw Tamara's stone form.

Jupiter sealed the room in his electricity force field.

"Ah ha! Confirmation what this demon says is true," Pluto said, tilting his chin toward Tamara.

"What demon?" Juno asked. "You mean the man?"

"Yes, the man," Pluto said. "He will become a demon soon enough. It is one of my favorite punishments, to make those who cross me turn into what they hated. This human reeks of concern and obedience. A few hundred years pressed into my service will turn him into the bloodthirsty, malignant human he's run from all his pathetic mortal life."

"Enough," Jupiter said, silencing him.

Tamara screamed in her head. I knew she heard the Dark King's voice beneath her. If she could look down, she'd see herself suspended over a scene of The Underworld. She must have suspected it. *HELP!* she screamed in silence. *He'll take me to hell!*

"You do not wish to hear my report, Your Highness?" Pluto asked in mocking tone.

"Get on with it," Juno replied, not taking the bait for a family squabble. Cornelius' hands shook as he readied his quill and parchment to take down every word.

"My scorpion scouts found this human outside Rage's vault, although even they did not know that's where they were. The human – after some physical persuasion – relinquished some rather interesting information about why he was there. He is under the orders of the Gorgons to release the Primordials. You are battling Gorgons."

"We know that, ya shadow-headed ghoul-wrangler!" Mars shouted. "If you weren't dredging your dungeons every day looking for more souls to corrupt and torture, you'd know how long we've known that, ya cave dweller!"

Pluto turned a cool eye to Mars. "Says he who floods my land with fresh stock, sending his war dead my way." Before Mars could respond, Pluto pointed a grey, veiny finger at Tamara. "If the Gorgons have chosen to rid us of this thief, I say let them do their work."

Venus stepped forward.

"Duplicitous words
from he so foul.
She, a thief?!
Didst thou not prowl
for a honeyed girl
to then deflower
and take below, despite her howls?"

"Who are you to give advice on love and marriage?" Pluto spat, looking her way. "I don't see Vulcan at your side. Besides, we do things differently down here in the real world. And speaking of down here, why is it that I haven't seen *her* yet?" Pluto asked, pointing at Tamara again. "Is one of you keeping her soul, hiding from me what's rightfully mine?"

Everyone looked at each other, perplexed.

I'm not dead! Tamara shouted in her head.

"I'll expect her soon or you will have trouble with yet another god."

"That mortal you're choking," Juno said before Pluto's threat derailed the conversation. "You said he is under orders from the Gorgons."

"As their sacrificial goat," Pluto answered, "their help from the outside." He turned his head to glare down at his catch. No doubt the mortal's heart nearly came to a stop at such attention. His heart would indeed stop just as soon as Pluto decided to make it. And he would soon. Breaching The Underworld is an irrevocable violation. It insults he who is charged with keeping it. It is a partial reason for my never breaching Pluto's mind. First, my living neebo could not survive The Underworld, cozied up in someone's brain or not. Second, even if they could survive, I would be guilty of an indefensible crime for assigning them to a mind as depraved as Pluto's. And third, the mind of the darkest of gods might turn me, the conduit receptacle, into a different being.

That poor mortal who offended Pluto was doomed for eternity. Pluto turned to him and spoke, his voice dredging from the depths. "You have the rare opportunity as a mortal to address the gods. Tell them what you told me. And leave out nothing."

Chapter 18

REWARD

The mortal shook in abject terror. He might have understood the difficulty in the Gorgon's request, but only now could he realize its ramifications.

"Speak!" Pluto demanded. "Or I'll have your intestines vacate your body through your throat."

"Ma-ma-my, my mistress, Medusa-"

"Your mistress MEDUSA?!" Pluto bellowed.

"Yes," Minerva said flatly. "She's still alive, along with her sisters. Her fake death was a stratagem."

Pluto squinted at her with calculation.

The human continued.

"I-I was chosen among her m-many loyal followers for the great honor of releasing the Primordials."

"Why?" Juno asked.

"Because I hadn't yet blinded myself."

"Say what?" asked Mars.

"Not why were you chosen," Jupiter clarified. "Why release the Primordials?"

"To create chaos, of course," Mars interjected, "but I'm more interested in the 'blinded' bit."

The human shrank, not knowing whom to address, until Pluto tightened his fingers around his neck. The tellurian sputtered, his rosy cheeks blooming in the flower of his youth. He seemed about 20 years old and very much alive, not the type seen in The Underworld, especially not by his own volition.

Pluto's eyes narrowed with a fury that said quite plainly, *Speak all you know.*

"The Gorgons' followers blind themselves to show loyalty."

"Wait, wait, wait," Minerva said. "Those legless lowlifes, the Gorgons, have followers?!"

"The Gorgons love us like no other gods!" the mortal said.

"The Gorgons are not gods. Bite your tongue," Pluto seethed.

The young man's body stiffened, except for his mouth, which stretched wide to allow his tongue to jut out more than should be possible. His teeth chomped down, and a muffled scream escaped around his fat, bloody tongue.

"We can't learn from him if you make him mute," Juno warned Pluto.

"And I should like to hear more about said blind devotion," Venus said, raising a handkerchief to her smiling lips.

"You already have devotion all around you," Mars cooed before turning back to Pluto and the human. "Tell us more."

Pluto released his power over the mortal who gagged at the return of his tongue and struggled to speak around it.

"You gods may hate the Gorgons, but they are our champions."

"Whose champions?" Minerva sneered.

"Champions of the unloved, the unwanted, the unblessed. The Gorgons protect us because you Olympians abandoned us."

The man's daring left no doubt that he knew he was doomed.

"Your curse," he went on, "turns all who look at the Gorgons into stone, but blind people can't *see* them, so they aren't affected. It was the blind who first discovered the Gorgons' kindness centuries ago."

"How?" Minerva demanded.

"During the old world's invasion of the new. European marauders stole two native sisters from their land and eventually left them for dead on Isla Gorgona. The Gorgons found them barely alive, their eyes nearly swollen shut from blows, moaning for help. They warned the girl who could see, the one who'd fought the men so valiantly to protect her blind sister, to look away if she wished to live. The Gorgons brought them back to health. The girls returned to the mainland only once for clothing, which the Gorgons could not provide. The old Tolita woman who'd sold to the girls asked where they'd gotten such ancient gold. The girls lied that what they held was the last of Gorgon gold.

The story spread, and several ships of Spanish conquistadors raided the island to relieve it of its gold. The invaders were killed, of course, their remains set adrift onto their ships as a warning. Imagine coming across a Spanish treasure frigate full of stone statues rather than weighted down with hoarded plunder." The man grinned as the image filled him. "For centuries since, canoes occasionally arrive on the island with one or two decrepit people inside, seeking protection from whichever society is hunting them for whatever imperfections, illnesses, or frailties. The arrivals gouge out their eyes as soon as their feet touch sand to prove they mean the Gorgons no harm. Then they crawl on their bellies until they're bloody and bitten by enough snakes that their new, loving gods take them in."

"How is it then, liar, that you serve the Gorgons and yet see?" Minerva asked, bending low over the ERP to get right in the human's face. "You would have been petrified."

"The Gorgons protected my pregnant mother. When my twin sister and I were born, they could not tolerate the idea of babies being blinded to stay there, so they gave my mother the choice to leave or stay on the far side of the island. We've grown under their watch. They rattle their tails to announce their arrival, and we kneel with eyes closed. They are charitable, loving gods to us, and I'd always hoped to serve them better. Today is that happy day."

Minerva stood tall and looked down her nose at

the mortal as if he were a leech swimming in swamp water. Then her eyes flitted. She bent down once more and asked, "How many of your type are there?"

The mortal grinned but did not answer. Pluto squeezed his neck, and the young man's lips tightened further. He began to turn blue, yet his thin grin held strong. It was clear he wouldn't yield more information in this lifetime. Perhaps after death.

"Why was this mortal at Rage's cage?" Juno asked.

"He'd released it," Pluto replied. "Just like his accomplice released Horror. The other human died right there of a heart attack, hopefully from distress, so I've set him up next to that cheat, Sisyphus, to forever roll boulders uphill. The strain has so far triggered a fresh coronary every hour."

Juno frowned but lowered herself to one knee, taking me along in her mind. She stuck her right arm into the ERP and swirled. Through that inset window, we saw the same Primordial at the Tibetan Himalaya. It was squatting, attempting to topple Mount Everest.

"That *is* Horror," Juno confirmed. "I couldn't tell before it shaped its mask."

Horror made for a grisly sight. Its body armor was bad enough, made of shipping containers spackled with vegetation and the dead created on its terrible trek. But its mask was hideous, made of chunks of broken concrete, no doubt from buildings crushed underfoot, held together by tons of mud. The teeth that were most terrifying. The concrete's support structure jutted down from above, forming a long line of jagged steel rods. It created an implication of teeth that could pierce anything.

Venus leaned in and dabbed at her eye with the handkerchief. "Vulcan fights," she said.

Juno looked closer, and together we saw the god of metallurgy flying with strapped-on silver wings. He led a dozen golden robots, each equipped with its own, golden wings. They zipped around Horror, dive-bombing it, reaching in to rip away bits of its armor. Vulcan spurted lava from the mountain's top, so Horror couldn't safely get a grip on the mountain's base to topple it. We also spotted an army of iron spiders, each the size of a cat, scurry toward the mountain. Vulcan's ingenuity never ceases to amaze. I imagined the spiders would scuttle into the armor itself and pull Horror apart, bit by bit, from the inside.

"Where's Rage?" Juno asked Pluto.

Pluto rolled his eyes in return. "I can't search for infiltrators here *and* find your many enemies above ground," he spat. "I've got enough work here. The mortal used the blood of a Gorgon hairsnake to burn through the Primordials' cages. He still had that snake. I'll be keeping it – perhaps to use on him."

Venus huffed and said,
"Thy cruelty knowest
no limits nor bounds,

nor dost thine incompetence quit.
Thou oughtest be finding
Primordials escaping,
not hoarding a snake for thy pit."

"What enters my domain is mine," Pluto said with finality, "and I stay here, too. Handle your own problems."

With that, the dark lord popped out of sight.

Habandash brought both fists to his hips, showing the frustration we gods felt but didn't bother showing. His employer's ERP was left showing Horror in all his awful horror and Earth a mess in his wake.

I realized we had to get Olympus in order in a hurry to have any hope of fixing life on Earth, but with multiple enemies fighting on opposite battlefields, we'd need a lot more to go right – and fast.

Chapter 19

NATURE

"Diana!" I heard someone calling as if they were at the far end of a tunnel. "Diana, wake up!"

I snapped back from Juno's mind at the CC into my own, somewhere inside Jupiter Heights. I was face to face with Cupid, him shaking my shoulders back and forth, making my head rock like a balloon in a hurricane. I slapped his hands away.

"There you are!" he shouted, spotting sentience within my barely-focusing eyes. "Where have you been?"

"Do not touch me again," I warned, not at all inclined to answer his question.

"What, are you kidding?" Cupid asked, raising both hands palms up. "You've been walking backward in a trance. We had to steer you. And now this!" He waved a hand vaguely around him. "I've been trying to wake you."

I looked around. We were in a bottlery. *Oh, no.*

"You might have helped me before we got here!"

I spun and saw Bacchus shuffling unsteadily between a series of emptied wine glasses set atop oak barrels. In one hand, Bacchus clutched a rubber mallet, a spigot, and a strip of fabric torn from his own clothes. He waved his other hand in a flourish, and a fresh wine glass appeared in it. Then Bacchus bent down and hit his mallet against a low cork in a barrel. Wine gushed out. He filled his glass and pushed the fabric and spigot into the hold. The imperfect closure ran red with gurgling vino. I saw the same janky setup afflicting four freshly tapped hogshead barrels. Wine escaped the leaky spigot, poured down the fabric, and spilled across the floor. Bacchus drank deeply, then moved on to the next glass. The king's wine would eventually drown him, to his gluttonous delight.

"This idiot's had a ridiculous grin on his face for the past half hour!" Cupid accused. "He purposely pushed through the snakes three times. I thought he'd figured out the right path to the Gorgons, but, no, he was just leading us here."

"He could smell it, dis wine," Jarel said, pulling on Bacchus' arm and slipping on the red drink.

The wolves stood nonplussed. Were they alive, I have no doubt they'd have been lapping the wine off the floor or licking it off their soaked paws.

The smell of this room was overpowering, sharp and sweet and definitely intoxicating. The wine's aroma was even stronger than that of the cedar planks that clad the walls.

"I bet dis is'a oldest wine anywhere ever. 'S priceless prolly," Jarel said, regaining his footing and tugging once more on Bacchus' arm. Bacchus shook him off. "He ain' gonna let it go. He gonna derail dis mission."

"He can't help it," I said, impressed that Bacchus

could keep such a pace of fermented gulps, but I doubt he ever had access to the king's booty. "He's the god of wine. He can't ignore his nature."

"God of wine AND DRAMA! Don't forget drama – which I knew he'd cause!" Cupid barked. Bacchus raised a glass in toast. "Between you sleep-walking and him sat-isfying 'his nature,' Jarel and I would be better off without you two!"

"Would you?" I asked, my anger triggering me to draw all manner of creeping creature toward me. Roaches, centipedes, crickets, all the loveliest little darlings to set an enemy's skin tingling, stirred beneath the floorboards and behind the tiles. I felt them, the multi-legged crawlers, rushing my way. "You believe you'd be better off attack-ing Gorgons, the very symbols of female rage, without a goddess at your side? Without, in particular, the goddess of the wild? Do you think she'd hear you out now, after so many warnings by seers to seek her out?"

"Warnings to seek her out?" Cupid asked, incredulous.

My lower-life-form friends spilled into the room, flowing over the ground and crawling as conspicuously and quickly as they could. Jarel scrambled onto the top of a barrel. Bacchus ignored the infestation entirely, as did the wolves. Cupid narrowed his eyes at me.

Turning more animals against me, huh? he thought. *She and Medusa playing the same game? In cahoots, maybe?*

I really might be better off out of Diana's sight.

Cupid's words bit, but I composed myself. "Begone, vermin," I said to the crawlers with a wave of my hand. "Your assistance is not needed, thank you. I am well." The subterraneous critters wiggled and hopped away. Bacchus kept on chugging. Jarel touched a toe back to the ground. I looked Cupid in the eye. "That Medusa and I have similar influence over animals does not make me her confederate. You have your responsibilities, and I have mine. Handle this situation, so that we may press on."

Cupid set his jaw and hurled ungrateful thoughts my way, but turned to face the room and Bacchus in particular. Cupid thought about giving the god of vinifera several warnings. *If you don't turn around to leave right now...* and *... Quit or I'll ...* but instead he raised both palms forward and locked his thoughts onto the wine within the barrels. I watched his eyes lose focus and his hand shake ever so slightly. Then a barrel twitched. Then another.

"Uh, Bacchus," Jarel said, stepping aside. "You oughta move out da way."

Bacchus ignored him. I stood back, as did the wolves, and watched the barrels twitch once more before they blew apart from erupting wine. Bacchus tumbled to the ground as the spirit he'd been enjoying hit the walls and splashed onto the tiles around him. Bacchus' eyes flooded in tears.

"What were you thinking?!" Cupid bellowed,

marching over to him and lifting him by his soaked lapels. He shook him rougher than he'd shaken me. "You're no good to me drunk. You can't help Tamara this way!"

Bacchus lowered his eyes and mumbled an apology that Cupid answered with a push.

"If you two gods don't want to be here, then leave!" Cupid said. "I won't even hold it against you. You helped me get inside. But I need – no, Tamara needs – real help."

"I'm going to help!" Bacchus wailed. "I just … poor Tamara. It's so stressful. I just needed an apéritif to … to steady my nerves." Bacchus howled and weaved across the room in lament. He was indeed in danger of derailing the mission.

"Bacchus," I said. "If you don't keep a clear head, you'll miss the opportunity to die as a great, artful statue, should that glorious moment arrive. You don't want to go down in history as a sloppy drunk, do you?"

"Me? A sloppy drunk?!" Bacchus asked with surprisingly clarity. "Never! No, Diana. I will be strong. For my dear, darling Tamara."

MMMMMYYYYYY dear, darling Tamara, you wanker, Cupid thought. He didn't say it, probably to not cause more drama. "I'm going now, with or without you."

We continued our search, walking backward, and I might have thought it hopeless had it not been for the constant chatter between Cupid and Jarel. I was amazed and impressed to hear them referring to my shield map, analyzing distances, consulting each other, and ultimately creating what could only be a mental schematic of the terrain they'd covered. I must have missed this while I psychoported.

"There are probably a lot of rooms big enough for three Gorgons to comfortably move around," Cupid told Jarel. His eyes widened and he stopped in his tracks. "Tidal waves of Triton!" he hissed. "I can't believe I hadn't thought of this. I figured they'd be hiding in the castle, in some corner room that would take forever to find. But, no. Of course not. If this is a coup, they'll have taken over the throne room."

Jarel slapped his own forehead in disgust. "Course! An' dey prolly need the extra space anyway for dey biggest snakes. You know, bodyguards."

"The Gorgons don't need bodyguards," I said. "They've got their own skills."

I saw Cupid's frown reflected in my shield, and I nodded back. We were becoming great friends, he and I. I could tell.

"Where's da throne room?" Jarel asked, breaking the silence.

"Ground floor," Cupid said. "Royalty never wants

riffraff traipsing all over the palace, so they establish their throne room at ground level."

"Same as yours," said Jarel.

"Yep," Cupid said without hesitation, "and for the same reason, although you'll remember that mine was more of a lounge with floor pillows everywhere. Tamara added a few upscale divans … before… " Cupid looked away and took a deep breath. Even so, his shoulders look diminished.

"No wonder da snakes been leadin' us up," Jarel said. "Dey jes' leadin' us roun' an' roun' while the Gorgons get more an' more settled in. Been nearly a full day since anybody ate ambrosia, too. Dem Gorgons can jus' wait fer us ta get all weak before takin' over."

"Never mind," Cupid said. "I'll search for them 'til my dying breath. Let's get down to the throne room."

"How?" Jarel asked, looking first at my shield for a shortcut and then down at the thick layer of black snakes below our feet.

"Hold on to your junk. We're going through," Cupid said, before lowering his free hand toward the floor. He spread his fingers and focused.

Jarel, Bacchus, and I looked at each other in alarm.

The snakes beneath us scattered so quickly it was as if someone pulled a rug out from under us. Our feet hit the floor's grey marble just in time to feel its vibrations and grab hold of each other – well, no one grabbed me, but Bacchus, still tipsy, fell into Jarel's arms like a tipping domino that failed to fell another. I grabbed Jarel's lapel just before the floor blasted away beneath us.

We dropped to the level below us in a raining cascade of pulverized marble.

"Whoa!" Jarel shouted as Bacchus overbalanced into him and pushed him into the wolves, who pushed back. I yanked Jarel toward me, and he – with Bacchus clinging to his neck – found equilibrium. "Cupid, how you do dat?"

"All rock holds water, especially marble," Cupid schooled him while chunks of rock and dust still fell, coating us in grey grit. "It's got a network of channels running through it, like veins, that trap water. I'm just setting that water free."

"Bravo!" Bacchus cheered. "Every good action-adventure needs explosions!" He was so covered in ash, he looked about a thousand years old. "Do it again!"

Cupid shook his head but complied, again and again and again, until we finally fell, with the greatest amount of debris and the most earsplitting crash yet, into a great hall that could have once only held a throne and its accompanying extravagance.

Now the place was dark and steamy. Part of the room was on fire. And we heard a whoosh-whoosh-whooshing sound that took me barely a second to recognize. It was the overhead, circular revving of a throw-weapon.

Chapter 20

THE SNAKES STRIKE

Mars' wolves snarled and leapt into the darkness before any of the rest of us registered where to go.

"Follow 'em!" Jarel shouted, raising his sword. "Wolves always go straigh' for da enemy!"

With that, he leapt off our pile of debris and plunged after them. A three-stoned bolas flew out of the smoke where he'd disappeared, its leather chords spinning, stones clacking. The entangling weapon skidded across the marble and dropped into a chasm created by broken flooring. I looked over the drop to see lower level rooms with walls broken down to create a cavernous network below. Broken furniture fed fires in each room. Every blaze threw angry red shadows against the walls and rubified master paintings set in ornate frames. The fiery flashes lit the glistening hides of so many, many snakes. The tangy smell of reptile and noxious fire burned my nostrils.

Jarel must have successfully hurdled the chasm because we heard his landing thud followed by a war cry.

Bacchus drew his own sword and shouted, "He today that shed his blood with me shall be my brother!" He launched himself after his new hero.

I grabbed Cupid's shoulder hard to hold him, but he shook my hand loose.

"Will you fight?!" he hissed, raising his shield and sword simultaneously. "For Tamara?"

"No," I said. "I will listen. Do the same," I advised and pointed in the opposite direction.

Coward, Cupid thought, yet he turned and jumped over a fissure toward the direction I'd pointed.

I turned and walked off the debris toward a jumble of overturned furniture. I sat on a ripped sofa. Not a moment later, a Puerto Rican boa slithered across my lap. I patted it before commanding it to alert me should the fighting come near. I positioned my shield on my lap, covering the two of us, and transported into Cupid's consciousness.

Tamara, Tamara, Tamara, he chanted to himself. I got his view as his eyes whipped back and forth across the inside of his shield, scanning for a Gorgon, any Gorgon. All we could see was rolling smoke and blazing hotspots. We felt sweat trickle down his cheek. We heard the wolves snarling in the distance on the other side of his shield, but we didn't hear swords clashing. *They're still hunting,* Cupid thought. *I won't fail. I'll find the Gorgons for Tamara's sake.*

"Medusa! Stheno! Euryale! Come out now!" Cupid bellowed into the room at large.

Sssssssss. Hissing broke out all around. The closest was to his left.

Cupid spun to his right to see the room behind him reflected in his shield. Red flickers. Bouncing reflections.

He squeezed his eyes. They were blurring from the smoke.

"You are not whom we sssseek," said a voice, low and slow.

"You're who *I* seek!" Cupid spat in return, shifting his shield in search of his mark. "You killed Tamara. Come by choice or come by death. Either way, I will drag one of you back to revive her."

A chair flew past Cupid, just missing us and crashing into a pile of embers that we hadn't seen through the haze. Sparks flew from the collision. An ember landed on a curtain and popped to life as a flame.

"Do you think we have not tried," came the voice, rising in anger with every word, "over centuriesssss of regret to bring our victimsssss back to life?!"

Cupid and I heard a clash of steel in the obscurity to our right. Jarel shouted. The wolves barked.

"You think we haven't ssssshed our blood," the voice continued, "cut our fleshhhhh, tesssssted potions, and ssss-sang incantationsss? Do you think we have not prayed to the uncaring goddesssss that our cursssssssse would be lifted and the dead sssspared?"

Bacchus screamed like a lady in a movie. The wolves snarled as if they were fighting a rival, roving pack. We heard a crash and tumble.

Cupid ignored their fight in favor of his own. He raised his sword and ran backward toward the voice. He swung, and we watched, amazed, as a disfigured face appeared in the smoke. It was clearly once the face of a girl, now deformed by the most horrid, reptilian features. Her nose spread across her face and extended forward, ending in a boorish blunt. Her lips were lost to a long, thin line. Her black and scaly skin could only chafe everything it touched. Her eyes, perhaps once a leafy green, were now neon, vertical slits. But it was her hair of course that would terrify most. What should have been youthful locks were now a wreath of quivering snakes, some green, some black, fat, skinny, long, short, giving her so many eyes, it unnerved me.

The transformation from human girl to Gorgon – a Gorgon! – was monstrous. And cruel.

Even Cupid paused.

In the instant, she disappeared.

Cupid raged at his hesitation and ran backward through the smoky hall looking for her. "Why hurt Tamara?" Cupid asked. "She did nothing to you!"

A sledgehammer split the fumes and smashed into Cupid's shield. He lost his grip. The mirrored dome flew from his hand and crashed onto the marble floor with a clatter.

"We attacked that demon Minerva!" The voice came from a different direction now than the hammer. Cupid scrambled forward to retrieve the shield. "That you and the Councsssssil interfered in our vengeancsssse only cost you *yours* and us *ours.*"

Cupid hoisted the shield back into position and looked around through it. Too much smoke. Too many red and black shadows bouncing off the scattered fires. "*You* lost? You mean your snakes?! You compare your pitiful snakes to my fiancé?"

"We did not kill your bride, god of love." The voice was moving. We heard the coils of her tail scrape across marble flooring.

Cupid kept shifting direction, eyes darting, sword raised.

"Your bride looked into the eyessss of my sssssister."

"Don't you dare blame anyone else for Tamara's dea-."

"I wassssss incenssssed by her death!"

The voice was near.

"WHO ARE YOU?" Cupid demanded, swinging.

"Medusssssa," the voice hissed. Her name hung in the air, disquieting like the troubled voice of a lost ghost. "Her death at our handssss was not intended, god of love, but sssso few are. Every death makes ussss more hated. Sssso the face of death is the punishment placed on us by that sssssavage goddessss Minerva, that zzzzealot made jealoussss because a god who wanted me more than her raped me at her feet, that hypocrite goddessss who sssss-corned the begging pleasssss of her priestessss, that masssss murderer goddessss of yoursssss."

Cupid's mind stilled even as he kept his sword

swaying behind him.

"Leeeave," Medusa advised us.

Cupid sheathed his sword and swept his hand around the room. What little water remained in the air doused every fire on our level. The extinguished blazes hissed heavy black smoke. Cupid's move made the visibility worse but at least killed the trick shadows.

"Our quarrel with Minerva doesssss not concern you," Medusa said, "excsssept that it will leave you with one fewer plotter in Councsssssil."

"I don't care about Council!" Cupid shouted. "I care about Tamara." With that, Cupid dropped his shield and sword. He closed his eyes and drew his bow and arrow. *Love hunts,* he told himself and remembered challenges he and his driver gave each other when searching for off-list targets.

I marveled as Cupid's senses grew sharper. His hearing picked up wood crackling in the fires of lower levels and Bacchus asking Jarel where he'd gone. But he honed in on one sound in particular: the dragging of coils across marble. Cupid turned and fired and, within the same heartbeat, recovered his shield to see if his arrow struck true.

Instead of a figure collapsing out of the smoke, we saw two vambraces cross and deflect the dart. Medusa's forearm armor returned into the smoke. A breath later, a half dozen arrows flew from the spot toward us.

Cupid dropped his shield and dived. We rolled, and I felt his stomach drop. He looked up, and I found us dangling, his hand grasping the edge of broken marble we'd fallen over. When he looked down, I nearly cried out. He hung over a precipice, centered over the largest fire.

"If you care for Tamara, asssssssssk the healer for help. We cannot fight the cursssssse ssset upon ussss."

Cupid slung his bow onto his back and reached up to grab the edge with both hands. He pulled himself up. Once he cleared the edge, he was careful to keep his eyes down. He recovered his shield and sword once more.

"We cannot ssssave her," Medusa said through the blear. "Minerva issss at fault. It issss alwaysssss Minerva."

Why didn't Medusa go in for the kill just now? Cupid thought to himself. *I was defenseless on that ledge. She made me lose my shield and then deflected my arrows, when she could have just stepped out of the smoke and attacked me with her face. It's the deadliest weapon here.*

Cupid's eyes, set on the inside reflection of his shield, lost focus in the drifting particles of soot all around him.

"Killing Minerva won't change anything for you," Cupid called to Medusa.

"It will for you, god of love and heir to the king-dom," Medusa said, her voice moving behind the smoke. She dragged a chain behind her, taunting us, perhaps luring us. Cupid inversely followed the movement through his upheld shield. "Minerva will attempt to ussssurp your power, as issss her nature."

"I don't care about pow-"

"*Shhhhhe* is the monsssster," Medusa interrupted. "Ssssurely you, god of love, see that shhhhhe cannot lead as a voicsssse on Councssssil. She must sssssuffer sssssome penalty!" A round of hisses broke out around us. There must have been more snakes on the walls.

Cupid headed backward toward the voice, sword held out in defense.

"Jarel!" Bacchus called in the distance. A duo of snarls answered to help.

A memory from centuries past flooded Cupid's mind: he, just a toddler, his father standing tall over him, initiating the first of many barely heard lessons in warcraft. *A distracted soldier is a dead soldier, son.*

Cupid nodded from the faded recollection and leaned down to put his shield and sword quietly at his feet. He closed his eyes once more and drew his bow and arrow. *I can hit anyone with an arrow,* he said to himself. *Anyone, anywhere.*

He turned toward the voice and spoke, hoping to elicit a response. "An exile is in no position to make demands."

"We will sssssiege until every Celessssstial is ssssstarved or turned to ssstone," Medusa said.

Cupid honed in from the first word and let loose

a low-aimed arrow, hoping to maim rather than kill. He didn't know whether a live Gorgon offered more chances to heal Tamara.

Medusa cried out, but we didn't hear a thud from her collapse. A moment later an arrow shot out from the smoke and ran through Cupid's thigh. He buckled as the searing pain rippled up his side. I'd never been hit by an arrow and just barely managed to stop myself from crying out and revealing my presence. Cupid hobbled away to provide some distance.

"You cannot hate ussss, god of love," Medusa said, her voice hitching from pain. "Not you. You musssst undersssstand. We demand our curssssses be lifted, that our followers be made whole. We demand that Minerva and Neptune be punisssshed. And we demand that you, Cupid, as Olympussssss' future king, defend mortal women from the abusssssses of the godsssssss."

Cupid gripped his thigh tightly, but we saw it was a clean wound, hardly bleeding, and well aimed so as to not inflict lasting damage. Cupid couldn't say the same about the arrow he'd shot toward her.

I realized Cupid was stalling. Thinking.

Defend mortal women? Punish gods? Who could possibly deliver all that?

"God of love, if you indeed do love, you will defend the meek."

Smoke billowed between us.

I felt a sharp pain in my forearm.

I snapped back to my body and found the Puerto Rican boa attached to my arm. It had bitten me. Without a moment's hesitation, I snatched him off my arm and lunged away from the sofa just in time to avoid interlocked weapons slicing down on where I'd been. A sword and hammer were caught together, their owners a blur.

I slapped the snake onto my shoulder. It wrapped itself around my neck like a scarf. I looked back into my shield to see Jarel fighting Stheno. I recognized her famed red hairsnakes. She and Jarel were well matched in skill.

The wolves were lost to the smoke and were no doubt helping Bacchus fight Euryale, the grey Gorgon who'd petrified Tamara.

A voice broke into my consciousness, an unspoken voice. Tamara's thoughts reached me. *M-my eyes! I can see!*

She can see?! I nearly asked aloud. I thanked The Fates themselves that I wasn't occupying Cupid's mind. My surprise was so great, who knows if Cupid might have sensed me? Who knows what he might have thought? That he was losing his mind? That Medusa was tricking him? That my disappearance from view rightly had something to do with it? Cupid's upcoming moment was too important for distraction. My seer's vision knew that he needed clarity.

Tamara's consciousness became stronger, and I suddenly saw through her eyes. She was peering at the high walls of the CC, looking up as she'd been when she was gorgonized. And though she could see, she could not move. She was still trapped within a cold, rigid body, and her desperate cries for help went unheard by all but me.

The wolves barked, snapping my attention back to my presence. Jarel and Bacchus shouted directions to one another, warnings. Gorgons hissed, along with true snakes all around.

I walked along the wall approximating my sofa, away from Jarel's battle. When I reached the farthest point, where two walls met, I stepped into the corner, facing it like a reprimanded child. I settled my shield's enarme across my forehead, and the strap gripped well enough to hold the shield behind my head, protecting my upper half at least. The snake slithered off my neck and up onto my hair, no doubt to keep watch over the shield's rim. I returned to Cupid's mind.

Cupid had entered the smoke where Medusa hid. *Where is she?!* Cupid questioned silently, sweeping his sword in angry arches. *Whatever Medusa wants can't concern me. I need her for Tamara's sake. Curse this Gorgon!*

He stopped himself short. *But she already is. Cursed.*

"If you still will not help ussssss," Medusa whispered, startlingly near, "then leave usssss be. We will fight and die defending our own honor."

Cupid didn't swing his sword, although it might have connected. *Not one of these Gorgons will come with me alive,* Cupid thought to himself, *not to be taken anywhere near Minerva. But if I kill them, it won't be self-defense, not like the last times I defended the kingdom.*

"Cupid!   Have you got one yet?" Jarel hollered. "Mine's as slippery as a snake. Can' getta holda her!"

They're leaving me no choice. But can I – me, the god of love – commit murder?

"Vines won't hold mine!" Bacchus half screamed. We heard him trip over debris and cry out.

And if I killed someone else, even a Gorgon, to bring Tamara back to life, would she ever forgive me? Would Tamara ever look at me the same again?

"Cupid, we're running outta time!" Jarel shouted.

As urgency registered, as panic for his friends and fear for his bride overwhelmed him, Cupid bellowed into the smoke, "Meduuuuuuuusa! I'll take your head!"

He regretted his words the moment they escaped his mouth.

All three Gorgons hissed and charged. We heard their sliding scales, felt their ominous rush toward us. Cupid looked into his shield to see them and their sledge-hammers flying ahead, already honing in on him.

Jarel and Bacchus called out that they were coming. The wolves' huffs confirmed.

But they'd be late.

Cupid turned around with eyes closed, pulling his shield in an arc in front of his body. The shield deflected the hammers but could not stop the second wave of attack. He was hit hard by three Gorgons hell bent on annihilating their assassin. He couldn't open his eyes to defend himself.

As fast as snakes can strike, the Gorgons wrapped Cupid in their coils. They squeezed. I felt air leave his lungs. I felt his chest contract.

Cupid writhed uselessly, his arms now pinned to his side, his elbows digging in to his side and further restricting his breath.

This was not how I'd seen this moment go. This was not right, not according to my vision. I was a moment from interceding, somehow, some way, when I felt a surge of power through Cupid unlike anything I'd imagined.

The snake coils enveloping him shook hard before prying away from him as if by the Gorgons' will. But we knew this was not their will.

Cupid fell to the ground, gasping for breath and rubbing his side. He picked up his shield. When he looked for the Gorgons through its reflection, he found that he knew exactly where they'd be, in the position he wanted, although he didn't know why. The Gorgons were fixed aloft, above the ground, alive but immobile. Even the snakes on their head were rigid, petrified but not turned to stone, not caught in their own curse.

The Gorgons' wide-eyes held the same disbelief that Cupid and I now saw in Bacchus and Jarel.

Cupid ignored their faces full of questions. He

didn't much want to think this through. Tamara's life was slipping further into the past, he reasoned, and he had to bag the Gorgons to save her.

I launched myself back into my body and turned from my self-imposed time-out corner to hustle across the room as fast as I could going backward.

"Nice of you to join us," Cupid said to me with open hostility. "Now that you're *helping*, would you mind wrapping those up so we can get back to Tamara?" He pointed behind him at the suspended sisters.

I ignored his jibe as he had no idea how much I was helping and called all the flora in the building and grounds. I had them weave three nearly airtight yet roomy cocoons around each one. The finished product looked like green gourds the size of pickup trucks.

"We need all three?" Jarel asked.

"We don't know what we need – except that we need to hurry," Cupid answered. He ignored the questions racing through his mind, which I heard nonetheless. *What just happened? How did I do that? And how could I have come so close to … the unthinkable?*

We left the room with three mothballed Gorgons suspended in mid-air and first-of-their-kind cocoons floating behind us. A few moments later, we'd be airborne.

Chapter 21

UNRAVELED

The CC glittered under the mid-day sun and Jupiter's restored electric field. We were closing in fast, and Cupid's thoughts became frantic. *Faster. Faster. Gotta get to Apollo.*

I was becoming frantic myself. The cocoons were shaking. For some reason, the Gorgons weren't immobile anymore within them. Each Gorgon was tearing at the inside. They had fangs and, in the case of Euryale, brass, clawed gloves. Maybe they even had hidden weapons. I hadn't checked before enclosing them. I could barely keep up with calling replacement vegetation from throughout Olympus. It was flying up to us, creating a drooping, green contrail behind our flying caravan.

I looked ahead. Cupid's giant white wings batted as he sprinted across the sky. Their blue tips created their own sort of blurred contrail. He looked and called, "Diana! Can you alert Jupiter to lower the electric field?"

The easiest way to do that would have been to tell Jupiter's neebo to send him a "hunch" that we were heading back, but how could I explain *that* away? So I drew an arrow. Even bouncing on the back of a racing golden wolf, I fired it perfectly into the stained glass window that flatteringly depicted my brother. The arrow didn't connect to the glass of course, thanks to Jupiter's force field, but the attempted breach would draw the king's attention.

Cupid saw the arrow strike and rolled mid-flight to fly on his back. He looked at us and spotted the incoming flora.

"What's happening?" he asked.

"The Gorgons," I answered. "They're shredding the inside. I keep adding layers, but I'm running out of plant life up here."

Cupid frowned, his wings still flapping as he flew belly up. His thoughts were so focused on Tamara, so jambled, he couldn't think straight. We'd run out of time and the Gorgons would break free if I didn't stem the attack.

"I'll constrict the cocoons," I said, "but we'll have to hurry. They might suffocate, and we want them alive." *And not just for Tamara's sake*, I thought.

My flora collapsed inward, per my demand, plastering themselves against their quarry. The Gorgons writhed, but they were stuck, their arms pinned, their hairsnakes squashed, their tails pushed flat. The mighty Gorgons couldn't shred my cocoon anymore. No Egyptian priest could have done a better job wrapping mummies than I did wrapping up the Gorgons. But these beings, unlike mummies, weren't dead. These beings caused death. And their wrappings weren't inanimate. The Gorgons' wrappings lived and breathed – and would deny their captives that same luxury in a decidedly short time. Soon the

Gorgons' lungs would empty and they'd be smothered, trapped in an immobile body, much like their victims. It would be fitting if it weren't so unjust.

Better, Cupid thought, satisfied, and nodded my way. He flipped over to fly straight.

"Jupiter will only drop the shield for a moment," I warned everyone. "And only at the doors, is my guess." I added that last part for Cupid's comfort, but I knew full well Jupiter's plans, having heard them relayed to me through his neebo. Apollo sent a flash of light through the window as confirmation.

As we approached, I saw a figure struggling in the plaza below, its feet caught in mud. Cupid's concentration was hot on the doors, though. I followed his gaze just in time to see the force field pull away, giving us our chance. Cupid lunged toward it, toward the possibility of saving his fiancé. The rest of us plunged behind.

Feeling the wolf drop below me was unsettling but thrilling at the same time. What fun it must be to fly on one's own! I squeezed my knees tighter around my wolf's golden belly and prepped myself for the shift from downward sweep to level glide.

The doors opened just before Cupid crashed into them. We barreled into the room behind him, we gods, wolves, cocoons, and all. We bounced against the floor, skidded across it, and collided with the far wall in a heap. Bacchus was the first to jump to his feet and pull his sword.

Jarel frowned as if he'd expected that honor. The Gorgons struggled but could not break free.

Cupid scrambled to stand and looked around. "We're not helping anyone down here," he said. "They must have taken Tamara up to chambers. Let's go!"

Cupid flew up the gangway, and the cocoons followed as if they were magnetized.

Jarel hustled to his feet and took to wing to follow.

I chanced a glance out the doors, beyond the small expanse of lawn we'd zipped past, to the main plaza. I saw something, oh ho, something my seer's vision had not anticipated, a possibility I couldn't have grasped even if I had foreseen it.

Oh, dear, I thought to myself. The gods will kill the Gorgons when they don't even need to.

I leapt back onto my wolf and kicked its side. Bacchus' surprised look showed he wouldn't have dared to kick that wolf, but he nonetheless threw himself atop his own as well. We held onto their necks as they tipped back onto their haunches and leapt up the inside of the façade wall. Their claws dug in and gripped tight for each massive spring upward. Each release sent chunks of broken wall showering below.

The trip up was admittedly terrifying for me. Despite the danger, I couldn't help wondering how Bacchus kept control, but to ask how the god of wine, the tipsy god of wine, keeps down his drink is, well, fruitless.

When we reached the chamber door, I was relieved to see that the inner electrical field remained sealed and Cupid was delayed. I ordered the wolves to go outside and guard the place. They leapt back down the gangway. I then sent Apollo a thought that we were outside. A moment later, the field opened for us.

"Wonderful. My arrow worked to alert them," I said.

Hmmm, Cupid thought but quickly abandoned his suspicions when he saw Tamara, still stone, standing atop an ERP which now showed two Primordials in quick succession. First, the Primordial Horror, sprinting over huge swaths of land, already north of the Caspian Sea and with each bound moving farther northwest. Vulcan was in hot pursuit. Then the image switched to the newly released second Primordial, Rage, stepping out of the Caribbean Sea onto central Belize. Rage's "foot" was black smoke, as unformed and chaotic as the rest of it. Swiping at that foot was a giant, blue-grey creature of the deep. I couldn't believe it. Neptune's Kraken.

I hadn't seen it in centuries, and it had grown far bigger since then. The towering creature swiped at the Primordial with its webbed, clawed hands and four tentacle legs, trying to pull it back into the sea, but Rage was still smoke, still a half thing.

The Kraken roared. Its chest and waist, that of a man, heaved. Its tentacled dreadlocks waved wildly. I shivered. Those tentacles could capture a ship just as easily as his four tentacled legs, which were capable of walking on the seafloor as easily as on land. Or the legs could come together to form a super-tail that could propel it faster than anything that ever swam the seas.

Behind the Kraken, half above the water's surface, Neptune choreographed. He raised and lowered his arms like a musical conductor, guiding the Kraken's limbs, but the Primordial could not be stopped.

When it finally stepped out of the water, Rage burst into crimson flames.

I suspected its fiery armor wouldn't follow the same laws of combustion as normal fire. And, I realized, if Rage had risen in parched foothills, it would have no doubt sparked a wildfire for the ages. Luckily, these tropics were perpetually drenched.

"Cupid," Mars said when his son walked in.

Surprised to see me – alive? Cupid thought to himself.

"Is that them?" Minerva asked, pointing to the cocoons suspended above the ground thanks to my command of flora. She pulled a dagger out of a hidden compartment in her gristle armor and approached. "Are those the Gorgons? I can carve their skulls off their spines right now. You'll have all the blood you need."

The Gorgons thrashed in their wrappings. I loosened a single wrap around each of their mouths just enough to allow in some air. One Gorgon's tail slapped hard against the floor.

The Gorgons are here? Tamara thought. *No! Don't look at them!*

"*Now* you're brave?!" Mars asked Minerva. "Now that the Gorgons are bound like mummies, now you'll kill them? Stab through their wraps like a great warrior, will you?"

Minerva turned on Mars with raised dagger. "*I'd* have gone after them myself but you and-" –she looked at Venus and Cupid- "*others* insisted I stay back with her." She pointed at Tamara.

"Lord, what fools these immortals be," murmured Bacchus under his wine –infused breath.

I'm okay! Tamara shouted in her head. *I'm here! Pull me out of this rock!*

"Apollo," Cupid said, waving him over toward the Gorgons. "Diana, would you please?"

"Wait! Surely you're not going to release them?" Juno asked, palms up to demand reason. "We'd need some protection from their curse."

"Well, Minerva could just remove the curse so we'd be safe," Bacchus offered. Clearly, he was coming back to his normal self.

"That won't cure Tamara," Mars said.

"Unwrap one tail, please," Cupid said, nodding my way.

If they had still been in their roomy cocoon, still immobilized, I wouldn't have been able to tell which part to unravel. But tight as these new cocoons were against them, just looking felt uncomfortably like a disrobing. The smallest, tapered end was obviously the tip of their tails. Higher was the widest part, what would undoubtedly be a woman's thighs, made lumpy by their famed sledgehammers hanging from their hips. Higher up, a tapering, a womanly waist, which I knew to be wrapped in chainmail under a backplate. The wrappings were lumpy against strapped holsters holding bows and arrows, daggers, or throwing stars. Finally, the head, made huge and irregular by cramped hairsnakes. The Gorgons' shape was laid bare before a hostile audience.

"Unravel," I commanded the plants at the tapered end of the central cocoon.

Cupid's neebo were silent and ready. Tamara's were scrambling with a hundred thoughts at once. Everyone else's in the room, those of whom I cared to listen, were unnerved. *Part of the legend turned out to be a lie,* Juno worried, *so maybe all of it is. Maybe seeing even a little bit of a Gorgon is enough to be turned to stone.*

But no one ran away. They all agreed with Mars' way of thinking in their own special parlance: *Better to die a stoic fool than live fleeing like a coward.*

The flora peeled away to reveal the ashy, circular rattles at the end of a huge serpentine tail. As the greenery shucked itself, the full breadth and power of that tail was revealed to us. It was probably five meters long, protected by segmented armor on its dorsal side, and muscular enough to contain any creature walking the earth today, even my griffins. This tail was grey and mottled.

Jackpot, Cupid thought. *It's Euryale. She froze Tamara.*

Apollo approached with scalpel in hand. With all eyes on him, I stepped back from the Gorgons, behind everyone, and stooped to the ERP. I swished my hand within to locate the plaza just outside. The figures in the mud were gone.

"Watch out!" Minerva yelled.

Tamara screamed.

Blood splattered across the far wall behind me, right in Tamara's line of sight. The red streak slashed across the white walls. As I processed the brutal contrast and the realization that I'd heard Tamara's scream – not in my head, but out loud – I watched bits of the blood take shape. Some of the droplets filled out to form wriggling red spots that soon dropped to the floor. I saw white within the red. Maggots, covered in blood, I was sure. This was Gorgon blood.

The sound of another heavy slap followed by shouting snagged my attention once more. I looked back to see Euryale's tail against the floor. She pushed off and collided with her still wrapped sisters. They dropped onto the hard, cloud-deck floor and flopped like fish.

Among the shouts and hissing, I managed to pick up the distinct sound of metal scraping across the polished floor. I looked over in time to see Euryale's tail land atop my brother's scalpel and wrap around it.

Minerva lunged for the tail. I caught the glint of her dagger as it came down with her.

And beyond them both I saw what an hour ago I wouldn't have thought possible. Barging into the room were Janus and Janice, in the flesh, not petrified in stone. They were very much alive.

Chapter 22

BLOOD FROM A STONE

At first, I thought I was the only one who saw the Jani – until I heard Cupid's thoughts.

My gods, they're alive!

Janice caught my eye, so I looked toward Tamara. Janice bounded her way, her brother defending their rear. Cupid utterly abandoned the chaos with the Gorgons. A second later I saw Bacchus do the same. We converged on the girl.

"H-how are you here? What happened? What are you doing?" Cupid was all questions. His neebo were freaking out.

Janice ignored him entirely and turned to let Janus do his thing. Her brother put his hands on either side of Tamara's face.

Her eyes! Cupid thought.

They were moving.

In seconds, color burst across her cheeks.

"Gods alive!" Cupid cried. He put his hands atop Janus' and squeezed Tamara's face with a joy that broke over me in waves. I stumbled back and slapped my hand on my heart. Tears rolled down my cheeks as I watched Cupid's head bob all across her face, kissing Tamara's light brown cheeks, her soft-again lips, the tip of her nose, and finally her fluttering, deep brown eyes.

"Cupid!" Tamara sobbed. She tried to talk through his kisses but couldn't get out another word. She soon stopped trying and just kissed him back, both of their faces wet from crying and exhaustion.

Janus kept his hands planted on her face, his head lowered and eyes closed. The longer he held her, the more color returned to her form. Down her neck it went, then to her shoulders. As soon as the color returned to her arms, they broke free from the stone and wrapped around Cupid and Janus.

She was talking so quickly I could barely understand her.

"Thank you, Janus. Thank you, thank you. Cupid, I could hear the whole time. I didn't die when I turned to stone. Pluto's after me, though. He wants my soul. And there's another Primordial loose, Cupid. And it's attacking Earth."

I don't know if Cupid was listening at all. He was too busy kissing her and thanking the Jani. His neebo were exuberant and confused. Hers were going berserk with how much information she wanted to share.

Bacchus studied Janus as Tamara's color kept seeping further downward. I wanted to understand what was happening myself.

Diana! Apollo shouted in my head.

I spun around to see him and the other gods

struggling to hold the Gorgons' tails with their bare hands. I don't know who could do such a thing. I doubted that all of the gods in this room together could pin down a single Gorgon.

I heard Apollo's thought a second before it was too late. He shot a laser of sun-hot light at Euryale that would quite possibly burn right through her tail, armor or no armor.

As if they knew their time had come, a still-bound Gorgon flipped off the ground to stand atop her tail. Euryale turned her wrapped head toward the sound and pushed in her direction. I saw the glint of Apollo's light hit the scalpel in her coiled tail right before she pulled that scalpel down her sister's chest. I heard the razor-sharp blade scratch into the breastplate underneath even as it cut and cauterized her wraps.

Euryale flicked her tail back on herself and cut through the plants enveloping her own torso.

"Shields!" Mars bellowed. His dais shot out of the wall, and a flurry of shiny disks flew toward each of us. I barely snagged mine before it would have cut off my head.

Nearly every god and Celestial in the room turned their backs to the Gorgons and raised their shields and weapons in preparation for battle. Except Tamara. She was still stone from her knees down, so the dais hadn't recognized her among the living to send her a shield.

"Keep your eyes closed, Janus!" Janice shouted.

"Keep working!" She had their shield turned to reflect her brother and Tamara. Cupid rested his forehead against Tamara's and covered her, himself, and Janus, in a purely defensive stance. There was no way he could truly protect them.

I turned and watched through my shield as Stheno folded her deep red tail to slide it out from the cocoon, as if she was shedding it. Euryale ripped the remaining wrappings off her face. The moment her eyes were free, her tail slashed the full length of the final cocoon. Medusa burst through the leaves, gasping for breath.

Chapter 23

PAST MADE PRESENT

pear!" Minerva yelled, and her weapons shot out from the wall toward her. When Medusa saw it reach its mark, she and her sisters lunged.

Mars and Jarel ran backward toward them, swinging.

Euryale sidewinded just as Mars swung past, and at that moment slashed both bronze, clawed gloves across his back. Mars howled and twisted his arched back. The muscular expanse was filleted, blood spurting. I saw white in the gashes, the bones of his ribs clearly visible.

Stheno dodged Jarel and bashed him on the side of the head with a sledgehammer as red as her snake scales. Jarel fell to the ground in a heap and moved no more.

Medusa charged Minerva. "Murderessssss! You've killed ussssss and everyone we sssssssseeee!"

Bacchus raced toward Stheno in defense of his battle mate, calling for his vines. But there was no vegetation left after my cocoons, and the vines in the building's statues were caught in the electric field.

Juno focused her thoughts. Her memory charm confused Stheno for a moment, enough to spare Bacchus from harm. But even I knew that her mind games couldn't overcome centuries of hate built up in the Gorgons.

Apollo dropped his shield and thrust both hands back over his shoulders toward Euryale and Stheno, momentarily blinding them and, unfortunately Bacchus, too.

"You shhhhhhould have protected me!" Medusa bellowed.

I looked to find her circling Minerva atop the ERP. The reflecting pool showed the Primordials' destruction below, but Minerva paid it no mind. The goddess jabbed her longspear over her shoulder, trying to gauge her nemesis' movements by the reflection in her shield. But Medusa had every advantage. The Gorgon spun on her long, green tail and swept its length under her foe. Minerva fell to her back with a thud.

Habandash and Cornelius ran to Jupiter's cubby and emerged chucking pens and mugs over their shoulders at Medusa, to no effect whatsoever.

Stheno and Euryale slithered along the walls, temporarily blinded. They darted when they heard fresh sparks of lightning headed their way. Jupiter was helping but couldn't risk electrifying the whole room lest we all die. The Gorgons, I knew, would regain their sight soon.

I noticed Venus retreated from the action. I read her thoughts. She never attended battles, as her beauty confounded *her* side as much as the enemy's.

"You shhhhhhould have pitied me and my sssssssuf-fering!" Medusa slapped Minerva's shield hard, trying to toss it aside. "Insssstead, you made us outcassssts, hunted for ssssslaughter. I begged for mercsssssssy, and you turned us into monsterssss!"

She lifted a huge coil of her tail and slammed it down. Minerva apparently anticipated it. She rolled away with barely a fraction of a second to spare.

I knew there was only one way to save us, all of Olympus and Earth.

"Janus!" I shifted my shield to the side to see him directly and the reflected battle behind us. "How did you do it? How did you break Medusa's spell?"

Janus kept his eyes closed, deep in concentration but whispered, "I am the past."

Color crept further down Tamara. She was nearly back to normal. Even her white capris and shirt flowed again, but she struggled to free her feet like the figure stuck in the mud in the plaza, the Jani, I now understood.

"You're ... the past?" Cupid asked, lifting his head enough to look at Janus.

"I see ... the past," Janus answered slowly, deep in concentration. "I make ... the past. I ... returned to the past ... before the Gorgons attacked."

I saw Janice smile at her brother through her shield. I didn't need neebo to read gratitude in that smile.

"Y-you can turn back time?" Cupid asked.

"Near time," Janus whispered, focused.

"No wonder I couldn't see this," I said, rubbing my

fingers against my temple. "I don't see the past."

I looked back in my shield to Medusa. The action seemed to slow as I watched. As she raised her heavy coils again to strike, I noticed not fierce rage on her face but the impressively detailed, rondel plates of armor on her shoulders. Someone, I realized, etched that metal, either a follower as an act of worship or the Gorgons themselves. I pictured these once-mortal women laboring silently in their exile, they against the world, beautifying an object of defense. I noticed the lames of their segmented tail armor, and I imagined the exiles of Isla Gorgona hammering metal to protect their defenders' longest appendage, their tails.

Then time returned to normal, and the tail slammed down. It pinned Minerva.

"Remove the cursssssse or I'll sssssqueeze the life out of you!" Medusa demanded.

A shield bashed against the back of her head, and I saw Mars in my shield without one of his own.

Minerva scrambled out from under Medusa and ran toward us.

Medusa turned to charge her. Euryale and Stheno joined her, their sight regained, their claws and weapons raised.

Minerva took a flying leap over us and skidded to grab a fresh dagger from a holster at her calf. In my shield I saw all three Gorgons converging on us, murder in their eyes, their arrows and throwing stars already flying, and we in the path of all their destruction. I processed it in a heartbeat. We probably wouldn't survive this.

In the same instant, I saw Tamara fall into Minerva, stumbling on freshly freed feet. Cupid's fiancé was no longer stone, but she'd die anyway, caught in the middle. We'd all die. I looked back into the shield and held my breath for the attack.

But the moment passed.

Nothing happened.

I tried to exhale. My breath was gone.

I couldn't inhale, either. Or move at all.

In my shield, I saw the Gorgons suspended in midair, their faces turning up toward the ceiling, their hairsnakes bending, sometimes doubling back against themselves rather than sticking out from their root of origin or toward us. I wanted to turn and look, but my body wouldn't respond.

What the hell? Cupid asked himself.

My eyes were set in my shield. I couldn't see him from my own perspective, so I psychoported myself into Cupid's mind once more.

The change overwhelmed me. His neebo were firing like strobe lights. They were focused everywhere, all at once, like Cupid must have been. I looked through his eyes and was amazed at what I saw.

He was wrapping his arms around his immobile

fiancé's waist. Tamara looked frozen again, but she wasn't turned to stone. She was simply stock-still, sideways to him, her arms stretched out as if she'd been regaining her balance. All evidence pointed to Minerva having pushed her off, toward the Gorgons. Cupid brought her into his embrace and held her softly, gently, extending the moment before lifting his head to look around the room.

Everyone and everything was suspended as they had been moments ago. The Gorgons' bodies were locked face upward, their gaze no longer a threat. Their throwing stars hung midair, neither spinning nor advancing. Bacchus was arrested mid-leap during another backward charge. Mars was running forward toward the Gorgon's backs, looking straight at us. Jarel was on an elbow, rising after that brutal head blow. And, *oh my Jupiter's thunder.* The king's lightning was held in place in his hand. Cupid's eyes lingered on that awhile. The king's weapon, arguably the most powerful in the kingdom, a weapon forged by Vulcan himself, was stayed by Cupid's will.

Cupid turned back toward Tamara and released us. She grabbed hold of him, steadying herself.

Juno gasped. Several shields fell with a clang. Jupiter yelped at the lightning shorting in his hand. He shook it loose, and it dissipated on the spot. Mars whooped. I returned to my body to see Tamara put her hands to her mouth, not unlike she did when Cupid proposed to her.

I noticed that Minerva was still inert, her eyes

pointed toward Tamara. I looked over my shoulder to see the Gorgons equally immobile, their faces turned up, their flying weapons suspended, all their action stopped.

Cupid would have no more of it.

"Well now," Bacchus said with a laugh. "There's a plot twist for you." He walked toward us to position himself within Minerva's line of sight, and hitched a thumb toward Cupid. "See that, oh goddess of strategy? No wonder it's he who's the heir."

Chapter 24

CHARMING THE SNAKES

"G rubby gods of glory!" hooted Mars, slapping the flat side of his sword against his bare thigh and letting loose a whistle that'd make any conquering general proud. "How in lords' light did you do that, Son?" He was stomping over toward him. "I could see you! You were the only one not stuck. You gotta teach me that trick. Imagine the civilizations we could lay flat with that power!"

Jupiter and Juno exchanged nervous glances.

Cupid ignored them altogether.

"TamTam, Baby," he cooed in her ear before dropping onto her cheek a kiss as soft as the brush of a hummingbird's wing. At least it looked that way. I felt like I'd intruded just by seeing it. "Thank the heavens you're back with me, my angel."

Her dewy, lovesick eyes reflected her matching relief. How much they missed each other. I looked away.

Venus stepped up and said to Mars,

"Our son maketh us stagnate,
as if held in a vice,
yet thou dost not ask whereby
arrives the device?
With a power so poignant,
dost thou even think twice?"

"Well, sure, I wondered how he did it, Hot Stuff," Mars answered before looking back at Cupid. "So what'd you do?"

Cupid was still kissing Tamara's cheeks and neck. Her neebo assured me she was elated to see him, too. Nonetheless, he looked up.

"I … just… stopped them," Cupid said.

Tamara's eyes went wide before she slapped her hands over her mouth and looked to Venus.

The goddess of love hitched the side of her mouth in a sly grin and nodded.

Mars guffawed and ran his hands through his thick, black hair. "Yeah, we all saw that, Son. But how?"

The Gorgons and Minerva held their frozen positions.

"I-I," Cupid began. "Oh, wow. I, uh, I can control water. So I, uh, well, I controlled *their* water."

"Aw, hell," Jarel said, and I didn't know if he was referring to a blossoming headache or the news from Cupid.

I couldn't wait to see everyone's reaction. Thankfully, I didn't have to wait long.

Tamara grabbed Cupid by the shoulders.

He looked down at her.

"Cupid, do you know what that means?" she asked with earnest.

I looked at Minerva. Her eyes were still trained on them. She'd have seen and heard all of this but obviously couldn't react. I turned to the others. The surprise on their faces – the rising eyebrows, the growing circle of white around their pupils, the loosening jaws – told me the implications were sinking in with them. I caught Cupid's expression just in time to see understanding dawn within him.

"It means," Cupid began, his eyes shifting between hers, "that I can, uh, ha, control a lot."

"You can control anyone and anything," Tamara corrected, slowly. "Every substance that holds any water at all, which is just about everything, Cupid, you can control. You can move it. You can stop it. You can manipulate it."

"Even disperse it," he whispered to himself. "I could tear a thing – or a person – apart." His voice held no small hint of fear.

"Son, focus on the moment," Mars said, really focusing on self, as so many do. "We've got a trio of snakeladies hanging in the middle of this room. We can exterminate these monsters right now and rid our worlds of them, both Olympus and Earth. I liked Minerva's idea of putting their heads on our shields. How should we split them up?" he asked. "You get one, of course, as a souvenir, I guess. I'd like one, too. I think Minerva's lost her chance at the final one."

I could imagine Minerva strongly arguing her right to a head, but as she was immobile, she couldn't say a word. That was smart of Cupid to keep her frozen. Juno, apparently, disagreed.

Juno stepped forward with the downturned lips and narrowed eyes that every child has seen at one time or another on the face of an ill-pleased guardian, only this one was grandma – and queen. "Cupid, regardless of what is happening here, release Minerva," she demanded. "No member of the royal Counsel is silenced except by word of the king or queen."

I held my breath and felt neebo all around the room do the same, their hosts picturing the many ways this scenario could play out. Juno's decree was more than a demand for respect or fairness. It was a power play, a demand for obedience at a critical moment directed at a god many times stronger than she.

Cupid looked around, assessing.

Cornelius raised his plume and parchment, ready to mark down for posterity whatever it was that would happen in this moment.

Cupid didn't move.

Pleeeease, Tamara thought, afraid to say a word. *Please, Cupid, don't be like so many others. Please don't display the dominance that so many mortals and gods alike want so badly.*

Mars hadn't moved either, so I dipped into his thoughts. *How in the uglies of The Underworld does my son end up with the power to claim the throne?* he thought. *He could destroy all of Council, all of Olympus. He could make slaves of whoever he wanted.*

Please show me who I know you to be, Tamara thought. *Please be the Cupid I love.*

Cupid finally turned, slowly, and raised a hand toward Minerva.

She blinked and stumbled toward the center of the room. But it was clear within moments that Cupid hadn't fully freed her. Her arms remained extended from her torso, the way they'd been the moment they pushed Tamara toward the Gorgons.

"Damn you, Cupid," Minerva seethed. "Release my arms."

"First we need to settle this with the Gorgons," Cupid said.

"By relieving their necks of their heads," Minerva promised.

"No one needs their heads anymore," I said with a hefty dose of frustration. I stepped into the middle of the room and pointed at my evidence. "The Jani and Tamara have been returned to normal."

"BAH!" Mars said, bringing the discussion back to himself. "What about all the other people they've turned to stone over the centuries? Maybe we can rub Gorgon fat all over them or something to bring them back. And then I can keep a head."

"It wasn't the Gorgons' essence that saved Tamara," Apollo said. "I didn't even examine the Gorgons. All I managed to do was cut one."

"And that blood is crawling," I added, "over by where your throne would be, Your Highness." I nodded at Jupiter. He walked over and zapped the maggots with a fire bolt before they had a chance to grow into something worse.

"Janus saved them," Apollo admitted. "Not me."

Janus stood tall and shifted to face the group. "Those turned to stone in the far past I cannot save. Too much time has elapsed. I cannot reverse so much history."

I wondered if that annoyed them, the Jani, one always having to miss the visual cues of a conversation while the other partakes, but I had to keep this particular conversation going. "So you can see, god and goddess of war," – I said, nodding at Mars and Minerva – "there's no point in killing the Gorgons."

"Those rebels attempted a coup d'état," Juno announced. "An overthrow. They must be punished."

"But they did *not* attempt a coup," I pointed out, an important aspect to clarify for the goddess of state. "Tell them, Cupid."

All eyes turned to him. His neebo were still contemplating his newfound power, but he knew his words right now mattered.

"The Gorgons told me they were never after the throne. They began the siege to force punishment on Minerva and Neptune. They want them off the council.

They want to be returned to normal. They want their followers made whole, too."

"These assassins, these transmogrified mortals?" Juno bellowed, waving an arm their way as if sweeping aside a cloud of gnats. "They dare demand the expulsion of two gods?!"

"Do you see now the need to exterminate them?!" Minerva squawked, twisting her torso as if the motion would break Cupid's hold.

"Cupid," I said, stepping up once more. "I suggest you release the Gorgons. Let them speak."

Bacchus immediately struck that same ridiculous pose as when Cupid uncovered Minerva's Gorgon-less shield: one leg back and he on tiptoe as if dancing through fields of flowers. As before, no one else prepared themselves for an eternity as a stone statue.

Cupid didn't raise his hand this time. He just looked at the Gorgons. Their torsos and tails rose to lay horizontal, nearly flat against the ceiling, with their hairsnakes facing upward. He released them. They writhed and tried to turn and push off, but Cupid had them locked face up. They couldn't gorgonize a soul.

The weaponry they'd launched earlier fell to the floor with a jangle.

"Juno!" Medusa screamed. "Minerva's a mutilator! And Neptune's a debaucher! No jusssst queen would tolerate criminalsssss in her court. How can a goddess – the goddess of government, no lesssssss – allow crimesssss to go unpunished?"

Bacchus dropped his pose but crossed one arm across his torso and rested the other elbow upon it. He tucked his bent wrist under his chin. The Thinker pose.

"Silence them, Cupid," Juno warned.

I looked at him, and he at me. He obliged Juno, but spoke for them.

"Your Highness," Cupid said. "There are only three people left alive who know what happened in Minerva's temple. Two conflict, yet one of them acted as judge."

Juno raised her palm to Minerva, ordering her silence before she'd managed to get out a single syllable. Minerva glowered.

"The third person," Cupid continued, "with or without consent from the mortal, knowingly desecrated the temple of a fellow god."

Mars picked up a sword, balanced the tip onto the floor, and pretended to lean against it, ready for any action.

"As for whether the mortal instigated anything," Cupid said, glancing around the room, "those actions couldn't justify such an intensely cruel and lasting punishment. And her sisters did nothing more than defend her, the way any one of us would for one another, right or wrong. So, as the god of love and a council member-"

"And heir!" Bacchus shouted, waving his 'thinker' hand high. "Don't forget heir!"

Cupid's expression said nothing, but I heard his neebo send a silent *thanks* to Bacchus. "-I recommend mercy to the Gorgons in their quest for redress."

"In their quest for revenge, you mean!" Minerva cried, disobeying the order for silence placed upon her.

"And wouldn't she be justified in that as well?" asked Jupiter, finally getting involved in this discussion of his kingdom. "Your petty wrath against that girl has caused quite enough turmoil."

Cupid smiled, and, knowing he'd swung the king to his side, really went for it. "I recommend the Gorgons be made whole again, that they be allowed to live their lives starting at their natural age before the curse and without interference from the gods, except for a nice financial start. The world has changed, and they'll need time to maneuver around it."

Minerva's jaw dropped and she stepped forward, arms still frozen forward, to possibly kick Cupid, I suppose. Juno held out her hand again, and this time she furrowed her brows in a way that clearly said, *Don't test me.*

"I further recommend the Gorgons' followers have their eyes reformed, their vision restored to its earlier state, and ..." Cupid paused a moment to think, "that they receive some of the blessings that might have stopped them from looking for help from beings like the Gorgons. I can provide love in their lives. The rest would be up to the gods based on their particular skills."

Silence hung around the room.

"What say ye?" asked Bacchus, hoisting one arm high as if lifting a lantern against the darkness.

Jupiter squinted at Juno, sending her a signal that no one else but the two of them could have possibly understood. She nodded and repeated, "Release Minerva."

Cupid did so. Her hands immediately sought weapons within her gristle armor. Everyone held their breath, asking more or less the same question: Would Juno allow Minerva to inflict the final punishment?

Juno lifted her chin and decreed, "You will lift the curse on these women."

Minerva balked.

Venus nodded and said,

> "'Tis the will of the throne,
> the gods' wish, oh so strict,
> That thou liftest the curse
> thou didst cruelly inflict
> on a mortal girl, weak,
> but so lovely at sight,
> that the mighty god Neptune
> chose *her*, not *thy* shite."

Mars and Bacchus roared with laughter.

Minerva looked ready to throw punches.

I might have called Venus' taunt nasty l if I didn't then see a tear fall down her face. She said to the room at large,

"Seek ye not a fair ending,
nor a fairy tale glow
for the mortals' tales, laden
with sadness and woe.
Pain. Tragedy.
Monsters and myth.
Gods' cruelty, lying,
assumed so forthwith.
Our history stained.
Mortals paying the price.
'Tis no way to show love
from divine paradise."

Mars and Bacchus looked at their feet.

Juno nodded first at Venus, then at Minerva. The goddess of strategy huffed and flicked her hand toward the Gorgons. The gesture reminded me of a gardener tossing seeds.

The Gorgons' backs arched before the startling transformation. Their tails shortened. Their rattles bent up and split in two to form feet. The split ran up their tails until the girls had legs again. Their overall color changed from green and black, from mottled grey, from fire red, to the warm beige of girls hailing from the Mediterranean. Their hairsnakes hissed before they thinned to the width of human hair, black and dusty brown and deep red, respectively.

Cupid lowered them to the ground gently to stand

on their feet. Naked before us except for armor that fell off their small frames, the girls were no longer a threat. I couldn't imagine they ever were, even back that fateful day. Medusa was no doubt a lovely girl in the flower of her youth, but no one could say she was a young lady whose beauty would change worlds. I wondered if perhaps we don't all see our rivals as more potent and threatening than they are.

The girls looked to each other with wide-eyed disbelief. I realized that they hadn't seen each other as mortals with legs in … ages. Each lowered her watery eyes slowly, as if scared her own lower half wouldn't match the human feet of her sisters. They stared at their feet. They ran their hands down their thighs, then shrieked and cried out to one another.

Minerva turned and crossed her hands at her chest while the rest of us in the room got to see a reunion that left us as teary as the vulnerable mortal girls. They took each other's heads in their hands and ran their fingers through their human hair. They hugged and sobbed and gasped their thanks to us as if we gods hadn't been the root of their evil.

I too had to look away, and, in truth, the girls deserved a moment to themselves.

When the joyful crying died, I glanced back at them to see three young ladies whose love shone through.

"Apollo!" Juno said. "No, no, never mind. Venus!

You, please, accompany these girls to Earth and set them on a new life. Heal their followers. Please show them the love we gods are capable of. Oh, and take their snakes along with you."

Venus curtsied in acceptance of the new mission. It occurred to me that Venus might gain followers from the grateful mortals. *Then again,* I thought, *everyone becomes her follower one way or another.*

Something scratched at council doors. Mars opened them to reveal his wolves, ready for the trip. Venus removed a few gauzy scarves from the many on her hips to clothe the mortals. Somehow the wraps became opaque around them. Venus and Euryale hopped on one wolf, Medusa and Stheno on the other. They headed toward the door.

Jupiter hit a fresh fire bolt against the floor with an accompanying clap of thunder. The electric shield around the building spit before dissipating.

"Janice, Janus," Juno called, "kindly restore those Celestials who've been recently turned to stone."

The Jani nodded and walked out, Janice leading them.

"Jarel!" Mars barked. "Take over their guard duties while they're gone."

Jarel saluted, wobbly, but grabbed a sword and shield off the floor and hustled out. His assignment might last days. Or forever. One never could tell when it came to working with the gods.

It was Tamara who spoke next, whispering to Cupid, yet her words carried. "We've got to help on Earth, Cupid. If the gods hope to have anybody left to rule, they'll have to fight the Primordials together, as one."

Mars whistled, Bacchus clicked his tongue, and Minerva snapped her fingers, I assume, to summon their transportation. I wouldn't be calling my griffin. I had no desire to advertise their existence to other gods.

Jupiter and Juno turned to face the wall, which issued forth their thrones. Their work would keep them here, along with their assistants, Habandash and Cornelius.

The rest of us grabbed various weaponry and shields and walked out to the vertical gangway. Mars and Bacchus each took hold of one of Cupid's arms for the descent. Minerva and I held onto Tamara, Minerva practically snarling in disapproval. Apollo dropped down by himself.

When we stepped out onto the CC grounds, we found awaiting us Mars' quadriga chariot, drawn by four huge black stallions, and Bacchus' three panthers. Bacchus waved one of them toward Jarel to help guard the building. The other he directed toward me. How thoughtful. Finally, an absolutely giant barn own came gliding in silent as snow. It was the size of any of my griffins but with a much larger wingspan.

The owl's wings and back feathers rippled

noiselessly in flight, orange-brown and tipped with grey specks. It was the bird's heart-shaped, white face, though, that arrested my attention. I imagined that face, bright as moonlight itself, swooping from the dark of a nighttime hunt and being the last thing its prey would ever see. The owl landed deftly and, from its clamped beak, dropped a grown red fox onto the cloud at Minerva's feet. What deference from Minerva's animal companion.

The owl's rest allowed me to admire the subtle beads, trinkets, and small animal skulls dangling from threads knotted into its neck feathers. Interesting that all of the threads were sized so as to avoid the decoration from clinking together and creating noise. It was then that I remembered. As dichotomic as it is, Minerva is also the goddess of crafts.

Bacchus bowed at one of his panthers as my invitation. I mounted it and assessed our group. We numbered fourteen: seven Celestials and as many animals. Such as we were, we took to the air to fight the most chaotic beings of all.

Chapter 25

FIGHTING NO BODY

The sun was past its apex. It was mid-afternoon with not a cloud in the sky, and all that sunlight made it painfully easy to see how much destruction Earth had suffered.

Without saying a word to each other, our group split in two, dividing our forces to fight on two fronts. Mars, driving his magnificent chariot, Minerva, atop her astonishing owl, and Apollo on the wing headed northeast toward Russia to help Vulcan battle the Primordial Horror. Horror would soon face two war hawks and the sun god, along with the god of lava. I almost felt sorry for it.

Cupid, Tamara, Bacchus, and I headed southwest across the Atlantic toward Central America. This was a hunt. This was my specialty.

The air rushing past us felt wonderful after being shut in the overcrowded and musty CC. The vast, blue expanse ahead conduced a moment of rest. Looking down, I was grateful for the beauty of white-capped waves. But I felt woozy. Exhausted. I wrapped my arms around one of Bacchus' exquisite panthers to take stock.

Less than a day had passed since we first saw the Primordials in Jupiter's ERP. It felt so much longer. And a full five days had passed since Cupid called on me asking to help him with his wedding proposal. Fatigue was setting in. My mind was clouding. Whenever that happened, my visions became less reliable. It worried me, but there was not a thing I could do about it. I had to be available to help, to see this thing through.

As I focused on the blue swells surging far below me, I noticed changes in color that I soon recognized as movement under the surface. They were shapes, rising and dipping. I took a wider view to see that the shapes were whales. Below them, I thought I saw the slower pumping of jellyfish. There weren't enough of any of them to call their advance an invasion, but I knew they were being summoned. Neptune was readying for the moment when he got the Primordial Rage back into the water.

My rest was short lived. We were soon honing in on Belize. Just offshore, the Kraken was throwing a fit, sweeping his arms across the water and slapping his tentacles onto the surface. He was furious that his prey had escaped. Mortals on the beach pointed, some at the Kraken and some at a trail of destruction leading inland. They'd have to be dealt with. Later.

Following their cues, we saw that the Primordial had crushed buildings on the populated coastline, clearly on its way to the jungle interior. Closer and facing us – and the Caribbean Sea – we saw Neptune, tarried halfway out of the water, his arms up. He was undoubtedly calling marine life to him. I doubt he had much of a plan other than to be ready for whatever happened, which I suppose is the best planning one can do.

No wonder the Kraken was upset, though. I soon saw that Rage was still within sight, on land but seemingly caught up on something. It was flailing.

We dropped in altitude fast and so low that we grazed the water. Sea spray splashed my face. It felt exhilarating. We barreled toward the beach and skimmed right over it. I felt the heat change from churned-up sand to fluffy loam to the cooling shade of a dense and still widely uncharted rainforest. I was confident Bacchus knew that this was a premier jaguar sanctuary. His black panthers would surely want to linger.

For now, though, they kept sprinting, carrying Bacchus and me just a couple of meters above the ground. They rose and dipped as needed, dodging trees at a terrifying pace that I couldn't even register. I held back countless shouts of warning. Cupid and Tamara also raced through the trees at breakneck speed. I would have chosen to fly above all this with my griffins, and I couldn't help but think that neither Mars' chariot nor Minerva's owl would have fit in these tight quarters. I closed my eyes and tried to see their near future. My overwrought vision produced not a glimpse.

"WAY TO GO, CERES!" Cupid cheered.

I looked ahead and saw what had Rage flailing earlier. Ceres, that great goddess of agriculture, for whom every being in the heavens and Earth owes a debt, stood with arms and legs spread, barring advancement. She was calling on trees to grow right around the Primordial's legs. Rage's fire burned the mahogany and cedar saplings, but the goddess could keep up. Ceres controlled growth and fertility as well as harvests. As the vast majority of the world's food comes from the rainforest, Ceres was her most powerful here. She looked it, too. Her golden brown hair waved around her face like wind-blown wheat. Her bronze skin radiated energy. And she tied her earthy brown linen robe with a sash of woven grass still green with life.

Rage tried to move one leg only for the other to be wrapped in new growth. It yanked at the saplings with its fiery hands only to get its arms equally surrounded in entangled growth. The beast spit fire, but this jungle was far too soaked to be susceptible to stray sparks.

Bacchus leaned on his panther to run an arc around Rage. The god of wine raised his arms and called vines to join the cause. Cupid and Tamara banked upward, breaking through the canopy for a bird's eye view.

I was a bit puzzled about what to do. Ceres and Bacchus were already using vegetation against Rage. None of the rest of us could use our bows and arrows to any effect as Primordials live forever. There's no killing an original being. One can only hope to contain it. We needed to do that again.

A flash of fire suddenly blinded me. I shielded my

eyes but still saw red through my closed lids. Surely the entire forest was ablaze.

Stop! I heard Cupid order in his mind.

"Ceres!" Bacchus screamed.

My eyes shot open to see steam rising all around. I couldn't see either Ceres or Bacchus, but I also didn't see a raging forest fire. The moisture here should have prevented any fire from catching, much less spreading. I looked up and saw Cupid with his arms extended. He put out the fire, I realized. An unnatural fire.

"It's moving!" Tamara shouted and pointed further into the forest. I knew she was pointing at Rage, and I realized, instinctively, where it was headed. If Horror's actions at Mount Everest were any indication, this Primordial was planning the same thing. It wanted to level the land, lay waste to it, topple any form that gave mortals variation in their view, tear down any building that gave them hope in their abilities. I suspected Rage was headed inland toward Guatemala's Tikal Temple, a step pyramid built by the Maya more than a millennium ago. The slender structure also went by the name Temple of the Great Jaguar. Though it wouldn't rival a modern skyscraper, the impressive monument towered over the surrounding forest.

I leaned forward, and my panther charged. We ran past Bacchus. He was on his knees wrapping Ceres in broadleaves. She was badly burned, but those leaves had healing properties, and there wasn't a plant within miles that wouldn't give its life to heal her. She would be well again sooner than any of us.

We charged. I called for flora. The entire forest came to life to fight its invader. Yet it wasn't enough. Rage kept moving inland. The temple was within view.

A shadow passed overhead, and I looked up to see Cupid and Tamara, just above the canopy, charging as well. They were shouting to each other, too. I couldn't hear from down here, so I lay flat against the panther, held on tight, and transported myself into Cupid's mind once more.

"I'm trying, Tamara!" Cupid said. "It's not working!"

"How can that be?" Tamara questioned. "It's got a body."

"No, it doesn't," Cupid protested. He thrust a hand forward like a gambler throwing dice, and I knew he was applying his newfound power. I saw through his eyes that his movements didn't so much as trip Rage up. "I told you, the Primordials aren't made of anything real. They're a force. This one is rage, the emotion, itself. The Primordials create bodies to affect the world around them. That's why Horror was applying debris to itself, and this one is using fire as armor. I could snuff out that fire, but then we wouldn't be able to see where it is."

Cupid looked ahead. The Primordial was almost to the temple.

I forced Cupid to look down at me so that I could make sure my body was alright. I was still flat against the back of the racing panther. Vegetation far ahead was following my orders and doing its best to ensnare Rage, but that was no solution, and Cupid's power seemed useless at the moment.

Something slapped Cupid's back, and he checked on Tamara to see her too being hit. By snakes. Cupid looked around and saw two golden wolves racing ahead toward the Primordial. One wolf carried Medusa and Stheno. It abruptly banked to head back toward Bacchus. The other wolf carried Euryale and Venus. The goddess of beauty was pulling behind her a gauzy scarf like a wedding train. It batted in her wake, but not so wildly as a scarf being pulled like that should. This one was weighted.

Venus soared past Rage. When she got far enough ahead, snakes – thousands of them, brought from Olympus no doubt – looked over the edge of her scarf and leapt into the sky. So many showered the treetops that I realized the scarf must have been enchanted. They just kept coming, wave after wave, dropping into the canopy, where they disappeared from view.

I was about to transport myself back to my body. I thought I needed to be at ground level to see them in action. I was wrong.

Something rose in the distance, breaching the canopy, something living, bent but rolling upward, straightening. It was variegated black with spot of colors throughout. And shiny. It opened its hood.

Holy hydra, Cupid thought before I got to thinking it myself.

A giant cobra, formed of countless interlocked snakes, now blocked Rage's advance. The slithering superstructure nearly matched Rage's size.

The Primordial slowed. It turned to go around the serpent.

But a second cobra erupted from the canopy. Then a third, formed of its tiny brethren. The Primordial was caught in a terrible triangle.

Chapter 26

HELP

The cobras swayed, defending the territory around them. Their color changed as the thousands of snakes that formed them slithered within. Every change of direction Rage took, a cobra blocked. When Rage looked for an outlet, the other cobras swayed. It had to be disoriented, and Rage wouldn't know what the cobras were capable of.

I zipped back to my body to slow the panther and direct it to stay near the Primordial – but not too near. Then I hopped back into Cupid's mind.

He'd caught up to Venus and Euryale, the latter of which was waving her arms, seemingly choreographing.

"You came to help?" Cupid asked Euryale, his neebo reflecting his surprise. "You let the Primordials loose."

"We're … grateful," she said with an arm sway, concentrating intently. The cobras waved in sync.

"The god of love should understand gratitude," Venus said to her son with a light tease in her voice.

"Fine, you're grateful," Cupid answered, directing his next words to Euryale. "Why are you still able to control snakes?"

"They're grateful to us," she said. "We've cared for them and think like them." She risked a glance his way.

The moment cost her. A chorus of hisses brought

our attention back to Rage. It had managed to get past the super-snakes to set a hand on the temple's roof crest. Rage's fire charred the pyramid's crowning structure. I could see all the elaborate carvings of animals and deities turning black with soot. It wouldn't take longer than a few more seconds for the inferno to dissolve the entire monument.

I shot back into my body and shouted as loudly and fiercely as I could, "Trees!" My call uprooted cedars and whitewood and breadnut trees and shot them toward Rage's hand. They struck true but didn't make Rage flinch like they might have done to Horror, which had created for itself a hard exoskeleton of debris and would certainly feel an impact. Instead, the trees hitting Rage sunk in to its fiery hand, descending like a branch atop quicksand. The burn was fairly quick, though, and smokeless. No single tree would have made a difference, but dozens at once did. They and their ashes seemed to fill the area between flames, enough to make that one section tangible.

The cobras sensed it and attacked. Each lunged in turn at the ashy hand. One sunk in a hundred tiny fangs, the fangs of the snakes that composed it. They hissed as they sizzled in fire. Rage flared in anger, flames shooting far.

I looked up once more and saw the rest of our party arrive: Medusa and Stheno on wolf-back and Bacchus and Ceres riding a feline. Ceres looked singed but not too worse for wear.

Euryale was once more sweeping both arms in huge arches, guiding the cobras. Rage stumbled away from the Tikal Temple, toward a smaller pyramid.

I looked back. Bacchus was talking with his hands, gesticulating, excited. His gestures were faster than normal, and he kept pointing to Medusa and back to himself. I decided to listen in once more.

"No, no, she's got a great point," Bacchus said with urgency.

"The Primordials were imprisoned for being who they are, just like we were," Medusa said. "*Our* prison was isolation and loathing. *Theirs* was darkness. We knew they'd lay waste if they were freed. They became our unwitting allies."

"So, so, so, you see?" Bacchus said, shaking his hands in excitement and practically bouncing on his panther's back. "It's their prisons, the Gorgons metaphorically and the Primordials literally. People need options, Cupid, choices, autonomy. You take that away and you'll always have trouble."

Euryale grimaced. Some of her brunette hair was caught in spittle at her mouth. Her arms slowed. She was tiring. Her sister Sthetho noticed. She shifted the wolf that she and Medusa sat on and took over the conducting duties. Her red hair waved behind her. *These girls,* I thought, *have always protected each other.* I turned to see her handiwork.

Rage and the seared cobra were locked tight. The other serpents struck and weaved and ducked fiery blows.

"The Primordials have to be imprisoned," Cupid said with finality. "They can't be controlled. They can only be trapped."

"They don't need to be controlled if their prisons are where they want to be," Bacchus said.

Tamara opened her mouth in dawning and said, "That's perfect!" She flapped to his side and wrapped an arm around him for a half hug.

Bacchus smiled at the attention, and Cupid's neebo flared in jealousy. I almost laughed right in Cupid's mind. Whose ring is on her finger, after all?

Tamara looked back toward the sea and whistled.

What's going on? Cupid thought.

Tamara must have seen his confusion because she leaned in and told him the plan. I heard, of course. It was a good plan. The right one.

Cupid put a hand to his head and thought it through. "Yeah, that might work. And no one gets hurt. You'll have to go ahead of us and get started," Cupid told Bacchus. "I'll figure out a way to get the Primordials there."

As he spoke, a black spot appeared in the distant sky.

"Really?" Cupid asked, turning to face Tamara again. "You called Cerberus? Don't you think Bacchus would prefer to travel by panther?"

"Cerberus will know the fastest way to The Underworld and can sniff around to find the Primordials' old cages," she said. She turned to Bacchus. "You won't mind riding dear Cerberus, will you?"

"I delight in obliging you in whichever way I can, my dear," Bacchus answered with a bow. "I am your humble servant."

Cupid rolled his eyes but was actually pleased to see Cerberus bounding across the sky to meet them. *Good boy,* Cupid thought but didn't say. Huh. The pooch had apparently grown on him.

Cerberus was every inch as impressive as I'd heard. He was huge, the size of a house, black as night, and he sported three, no doubt fierce, heads. The dog used to guard one of the entrances to The Underworld, just past the River Styx. If someone didn't belong there, one or all of Cerberus' three heads would do whatever it took to protect Pluto's kingdom. The story goes that Tamara rescued Cerberus when she went down to Pluto's domain to spy. I couldn't decide which was gutsier: infiltrating The Underworld to spy on the God of Death or trying to win over a hellhound.

Cerberus stopped beside Tamara and nudged her happily with all three heads. I say "nudge" but Tamara had to push back hard to not get shoved out of the group entirely. The dog then licked Cupid, and several snakes fell out of its mouth onto his head.

"Argh!" Cupid yawped.

I looked beyond Cerberus' heads to his body and noticed that his belly was fully distended.

When the pooch smiled at Cupid's disgust, I saw a dozen or more whole and half-eaten snakes caught in the teeth of all three jaws.

I silenced my laugh lest Cupid hear it in his head, but it wasn't easy. While we gods had been struggling in Olympus, fighting a siege that threatened the kingdom, this dog was feasting. He'd gorged himself. He looked happier than any dog I'd ever seen.

Bacchus approached Cerberus on his panther. As soon as one of Cerberus' eyes spotted the cat, all three heads turned and snarled.

Ah, so the history I sensed between these creatures was confirmed. They did indeed once fight.

"It's okay, Poochie," Tamara said, setting both hands on Cerberus' side to sooth her pet. "The cats won't hurt you." She leaned in to whisper directions.

Cerberus tensed. He turned to focus all six eyes on Tamara. She nodded her reassurance, kissed each of his snouts in turn, and said, "Be brave. I won't let him take you."

Cerberus lifted all his heads high and turned parallel to Bacchus to allow him to mount. The panther approached and leaned in to deposit his master.

"I'll join you," Ceres said and also climbed up off

the panther. "I'll visit my daughter and see to it that these beings don't threaten her."

"Bring me my chariot," Bacchus told the panther he'd just dismounted. The jungle cat set off. I wondered why he'd want his chariot. He already had transportation at the moment. But I decided his reasons are his own.

Bacchus and Ceres patted Cerberus's back and leaned in for their cross-Atlantic sprint.

Cupid turned to look back at the fight sweeping over one of the largest archeological sites of the Mayan civilization. Rage and the cobras were fully entwined and stumbling about the grounds. *How do I get a fire elemental going where it won't want to go?*

Tamara tapped us – well, tapped him – on the shoulder. When we looked around, back where Bacchus had gone, we saw something else approaching: an iridescent bullet headed our way, about the length of a football, with transparent wings. Jupiter's buggy little messenger was speeding our way on winged sandals that recently belonged to Mercury.

I would have grinned had I been in my own body. Sometimes my ability to nudge people comes in veeeery handy.

Pip skidded to a halt half a foot before Tamara's face, bowed to her and Cupid, and said, "Cornelius sent me a parchment. He said you'd need my help."

Tamara brought him in for a hug. "You bet we

do!" she said.

Cupid raised a hand to his forehead. *Ay,* he thought. *Cherubs.*

Pip reached into his armpit and pulled out the parchment and also a handful of glittering dust. I wondered how he hid them there. Nonetheless, he shook the dust onto the note and shot it into the air. It disappeared.

"To report that I've arrived," Pip clarified.

Cupid sighed inwardly but said, "You, Pip, get to save the day."

Chapter 27

PERCEPTION

Please hurry!" Stheno shouted. "We're losing so many snakes! They're giving their lives!"

Cupid looked at the giants battling at the ancient ruins, bumping into the step pyramids of a people who lived millennia ago. Modern generations could no longer be put at risk. The people here and those in the path of Horror had to be saved. The remaining snakes deserved to be saved.

"Pip," Cupid said. "Remember Jupiter's gift to you for helping the kingdom? Your ability to camouflage yourself?"

Pip nodded.

"Time to see how far that knack goes. I need you to project the scenery around you."

Pip's eyes widened.

"You can do it," Tamara assured him.

I decided I was doing no more good at the ground level. I zipped back down to my body and steered my panther into the sky to hover beside the group, live in the flesh.

"Get ready to dissolve the snakes," Cupid told Stheno, who steadied both arms for her cue. "Now!"

Stheno lowered her arms, and the attacking cobras collapsed to the ground in three distinct piles of smaller snakes, many dead and burned. Those still alive scattered toward the relative safety of the tree line.

Pip dashed to flutter in Rage's face. Before the Primordial could reorient itself, Pip scrunched into a ball, shook a bit, and suddenly stretched himself out. His whole body depicted the scene behind him. He was the Tikal Temple and the rainforest surrounding it, in miniscule.

Cupid swung his arms toward Pip. Water in the air around us gathered behind him and curved to form a portion of a much larger sphere.

"Toss your shields to Pip!" Cupid demanded, concentrating intently.

We threw the disks as hard as we could. They hurtled past Rage and were almost at Pip before Cupid used his newfound power to shatter them into countless shards. The bits parted and continued around and past Pip. They attached to the inner surface of Cupid's semi-sphere. Soon, Pip's reproduction of his surroundings reflected onto them. Pip had become the projector for a giant reflective screen behind him – a screen, coincidentally, that was shaped like a shield. For all Rage knew, it was looking back into the forest, this time without interfering cobras.

"We won't travel with you," Medusa said. "Not over the sea where Neptune stands." I looked over and saw her and her sisters bow to Cupid the best they could over the backs of Mars' wolves, but Cupid didn't see. He was concentrating on keeping his new screen together.

"Good luck, god of love. And thank you."

Cupid nodded, still not looking at them, and I saw Venus turn the two wolves toward the South. She would settle the mortals nearby then, in Central or South America.

"Mr. Cupid!" Pip shouted. "I don't like this!"

I looked back to see the reflective shield heading to sea. Pip's sandaled feet were sprinting toward it, toward the Mediterranean and Cape Matapan, the same portal to The Underworld that Tamara had used on her dreadful trip. The Primordial was lumbering toward Pip, trying to grab hold of and destroy the temple projected on his body. The semi-sphere led the pace ahead of them both, and we Celestials raced behind it all.

I knew we'd have no time to lose on the beach. It was late afternoon, and we'd lose daylight even faster as we headed east. I couldn't get out ahead, though.

As soon as we were over open water, I felt what I dreaded: the splash of spray as the Kraken swiped opposing tentacles through Cupid's semi-sphere. The configuration fell apart, and its projected temple disappeared. The spell on the Primordial was broken. The monster was free.

Cupid and Tamara shouted something at Pip.

I chose to deal with the Kraken. I drew an arrow, pulled it tight against my bow's string, and fired the screaming dart.

The beast roared when my arrow ran him through.

He flailed his tentacles and tore his claws across the sky, toward me. Neptune bellowed in anger. I looked down at him.

"Let us pass, Neptune!" I shouted.

The god of the sea rode beside the Kraken in a chariot made of a hollowed, polished conch shell. The shell was pulled by white horses whose hooves just skimmed the waves. Neptune looked imposing as always with his flowing white hair and beard. His light-skinned chest was exposed, muscular as ever. He covered his shoulders in armor made of pearlescent white-coral. Green, blue, and purple scales began just under his massive pecs and trailed down to protect him from waist to knees and again at his forearms. His mesmerizing cape rippled behind him. It was nearly see-through except for shining, undulating lights of bioluminescence. It wasn't as pretty as it sounds. Neptune puts the fear of gods into anyone, and he looked enraged.

"How dare you attack my guard?" he howled.

"We have the Primordial!" I explained. "Make way!"

I pointed to Rage and saw it being splashed with water from whale flukes. I knew instinctively those were the same whales I'd seen on our way here, sent to douse Rage's fire or maybe put their weigh on the Primordial and sink it once the Kraken dragged it below the surface. The Kraken wasn't having much luck, though. his claws swept right through Rage's wispy body. Perhaps the next best hope was an army of jellyfish awaiting as the rearguard. They had circled the group, their tentacles spread out away from the action in case Rage stumbled onto the surface a bit out of the way. The jelly's feelers were primed to sting and ensnare despite their shimmering beauty. The most hair-thin of them looked like the iridescent lines in soap bubbles.

"Make way, Neptune!" I demanded once more. "The king's messenger guides the beast, and Cupid contains it!"

I hated having to evoke Pip and Cupid as my license to pass, but I didn't have time to educate my uncle on the rights of other gods to pass through domains unfettered. Technically, Neptune controlled the seas and all air, but of course he could only get territorial about the air *over* his seas. Still, that's most of Earth. Cutting through the red tape here was my only time saver – and the royal messenger and king's heir were privileged travelers.

Neptune lifted his golden trident and slapped it onto the water. The impact produced an echoing boom that triggered the Kraken, whales, and jellyfish to still themselves before slipping back below the surface.

Pip zipped in front of Rage to recapture his attention. Once Cupid restored the semi-sphere, we sprinted unmolested to the gates of The Underworld.

We were pleased to see Cerberus emerge from a cave in the bay. Everyone prepared to descend, but I stopped us and surprised everyone by offering to stay behind, outside, with Tamara. She balked, as I expected she would.

"Take a moment, Tamara, to think this through," I warned her. "You might not be well received. You, being alive. Flaunting that status might tempt Pluto to change it."

"Diana, with respect," Tamara began, – and I did indeed hear her neebo emit respect – "I intend to go into the Underworld. I can't avoid flaunting my status among the living. I'm alive. Pluto's not liking that is his problem. He doesn't have the authority to nab the living, even if they're entering The Underworld so long as they're on official business, which this is. And Cupid and I are a team. We'll see this through together."

Cupid's neebo transmitted worry but pride for her moxie. He smiled at her, and we crossed into The Underworld.

I'd heard that the path to the land of the dead is dark and mystifying. I wondered if those few beings who'd escaped the Underworld simply forgot how they'd managed it, what with the fog of death around them. Now I understood. An incomer was drawn in to their own obliteration, hypnotized by shadows and cliffs.

"Hold on to Cerberus," Tamara warned us. We all put a hand on him. Even the panthers brushed alongside him. I looked for landmarks but strained to see anything. I soon lost my focus.

In what seemed like only moments, Cerberus

nudged us. I shook my head and refocused. *Son of a centaur!* I thought. We'd traveled. A lot. Only Cerberus knew how far. And only he knew the way back. Had my vision shown me this vulnerable state, I'd have resolved to leave a trail for escape.

I looked around and held back a gasp of recognition. We were in a large cavern, the near twin of the one I'd seen through the bat's vision days ago. Like that space, this one housed a cage with bars, its door wide open. Inside, the semi-sphere led a race around the inside bars. Pip was placing second, his color adjusting faster than disco lights, and the Primordial was third, right at Pip's heels.

Bacchus didn't look concerned. He stooped beside the door pulling theatrical trappings out of the silver reliefs on the sides of his chariot. He dug an arm into the relief and pulled out a purple velvet curtain, at least 15 feet long. It trailed behind him as he carried it through the door and disappeared within.

"How do those flimsy bars hold back such a creature?" asked a voice to our left. We turned to find Ceres in the shadows. She'd made thin lines of her lips. She looked distinctly annoyed. "Or is it another trick by that horrid son-in-law of mine?"

No one answered. What could we say? She was right that her son-in-law was horrid. No one would make a worse son-in-law than Pluto, even without considering the circumstances of her daughter's nuptials. And we didn't really know just what we saw down here that might be a trick of his – or a curse. It could all be.

Bacchus must have hung his curtain because we lost sight of the cage's interior. Luckily, Pip zoomed out of the cage. He headed straight for us with a look of pure terror on his face even though the Primordial was no longer on his heels. Bacchus stepped out of the cage blithely, snapped its door shut, and stepped into his carriage. His panther flew him our way.

"He wouldn't let me see her, you know," Ceres huffed. "My own daughter! Imagine! He said it wasn't time yet, that I had a 'lively' affect on her that clashed with the theme of his domain." She snuffed. "I bet."

Bacchus landed square in front of us and changed the subject without knowing. "I am enchanted by this challenge," he said. "And it was inspired, if I do say so myself. Well, it was Medusa who gave me the idea," he explained.

Pip must have had a curious look on his face – well, he knew nothing of the plan – because Bacchus directed his next words at him.

"Medusa and the Primordials suffered similarly," Bacchus explained. "They were exiled, secluded, and left to live a tragedy. The mortal girls now have a chance at life. May it be worthy of ovation. The Primordials' existence, however, must be contained. But how to contain them without engendering a desire for escape and revenge? Why, the answer of course, is to offer them their best world. Theatre, entertainments, our illusions, they keep the mind active. The Primordials' new home will be the largest continuous show of theatre I will have ever put on, creating within their cages the life each desires.

"Even Medusa agreed that this was the most compassionate life for them. As we speak, Rage is happily – or ragily? – toppling buildings I've constructed within. Oh, the sets I'll build! The sound systems I'll engineer! The storylines I'll imagine!

"Come! Let's get Horror! I've got whole landscapes, complete with mountain peaks, ready in *his* virtual world!"

I couldn't see the future any more. Not today. My intellectual power was drained, although my physical stamina carried on.

Cerberus led us out of The Underworld, and we traveled to Moscow. There, we found Horror yanking on one of the candy-colored onion domes atop Saint Basil's Cathedral in Red Square. The brightly patterned caps make for one of the most charming attractions in the world. They're bulbous at the bottom, pointy at the top, just like onion, and they've topped nine of the building's column-like drums for four and a half centuries. Such a delightful structure would be a natural target for an elemental bent on destruction.

Trying to stop it were Mars, Minerva, Apollo, Vulcan, Cupid's former driver Tyrone, and a lady love angel whom I didn't recognize.

Vulcan's robotic spiders were likely causing as much damage to the building as Horror itself in their attempt to pull away his armor. Tyrone and his friend were completely ineffective with their love arrows. Still, one couldn't help but admire their spirit. Only Apollo and the war gods were having a real impact. Apollo burned holes in the armor through which Mars and Minerva heaved axes. Those weapons blew out armor on Horror's far side. Those blows, in turn, buried axes and debris into the monument, which was unfortunate.

Our group didn't bother to explain. Pip flew daringly right into Horror's face and shone his beautiful, reflective self. Cupid did his trick, and, as the creature began its charge toward captivity, we got to witness the surrounding gods' stupefaction at being bested at the job by a cherub that resembled a bug.

Within the hour, we'd deposited Horror into The Underworld the same way we had Rage. Only, during this incursion, Pluto was waiting for us.

The God of the Dead materialized out of the darkness, tall and gaunt as usual, his skin nearly grey from lack of sunlight. His flowing, black robes seemed to disappear at the edges as if he was only halfway here. But he was here, alright.

"I understand this is the second time today you've invaded my kingdom," Pluto said to Tamara, ignoring the rest of us. "Weren't you recently dead? Did someone bring you back to life and deprive me of my prize?"

Tamara didn't move. She didn't look directly at him, either. That was smart. Staring death in the eye must surely harm the psyche. "I wasn't dead," she answered.

Cupid stepped toward her, but the dark lord anticipated his interference. Pluto swished his robes. An impenetrable darkness enveloped us, cold as ice. I tensed as I felt Cupid seize my body, well, the water within it, and quickly release me. I knew he was doing this all around, searching for Pluto, but the king of shadows might have protections here. I simply didn't know.

"Are you here to steal from me again, love angel?" Pluto asked. His voice seemed to be moving.

I heard swords unsheathe and muffled demands to be released. The darkness dampened all voices but his.

"You're free to go," Pluto said. "But not this one. This Celestial will labor in my fields, dig my mines, do whatever unpleasant task I need of her until she's repaid her debt. You see, this one owes me for blowing up my home, and I intend to collect."

"Oh, puh-lease," said a voice crisp and clear through the cover. "That castle was even uglier than the one we co-habitate now. We should be thanking this girl for rubbing it off the face of The Underworld."

The darkness swirled and disappeared as a woman, swishing her own black robes, came into view. She dropped the fabric, and it swung back to form a shiny, silk gown embroidered with roses and edged in lace, everything black. She donned a black Spanish peineta hair comb in her upswept blonde hair. She looked pale, too, which meant she'd been here awhile, but the flowers could only mean one thing. This was Proserpina, Ceres' daughter, and Queen of The Underworld.

She dropped a kiss on Tamara's cheek. It startled her and left a black mark with spider veins that crept out before withdrawing. The mark disappeared in an instant. Tamara stayed still. So did the rest of us, except Bacchus of course. He couldn't hold back a wide smile. This was too wonderful a turn of events for him to not enjoy.

"You must be Tamara," Proserpina said. "I've heard so much about you." She shot a hateful look at Pluto. "Well, anyone or anything that upsets my macabre husband as much as you have has my support."

Pluto raised his index finger like a father about to berate a child. But just then Ceres stepped out of the shadows and crossed her arms at him. Pluto stilled.

"You're welcome any time you'd like to help Bacchus here keep up the prison. All of you. Apparently the job was too taxing for my bitter half."

"Your bitter half," Pluto seethed, lowering his face

to within an inch of Proserpina's, "is relieved to see one of Jupiter's dirty tasks foisted on someone else for a change."

The queen turned and waved a hand in front of her face as if she disapproved of Pluto's breath. A black lace fan appeared, and she continued the job with it. She directed her next words at Bacchus. "You'll have to forgive Pluto. He's endlessly complaining about his responsibilities. He would have you believe that reigning over a kingdom is a burden. But at least he'll no longer have to house the Primordials." She nodded at Bacchus. "I'm sure you'll do a better job of it."

She turned and wrapped her arm around Pluto's arm, tight against his side, and extended her free hand toward her mother, who of course took hold. "Come now, Loves, let's leave these great champions to enjoy their success, up on the surface, where I will be in just a few short weeks. I'm sure you'll miss me," she said to Pluto, who scowled more than usual, "won't you, Boopsie?" Smoke surrounded them before being swept away, they along with it.

Bacchus and Mars roared in laughter. Cupid and Minerva shushed them, even though they themselves giggled. Still. Best not to have Pluto hear laughter directed at him echo across his dismal domain.

The animals with us began scratching the ground. I knew they didn't like it here.

"Are we done?" Cupid asked.

"Oh, yes," Bacchus said, rolling back and forth on

his heels. "This is stupendous work."

He was fair in his self-assessment. I don't believe the god of drama had ever enjoyed himself so much, except perhaps during his previous adventure with Tamara. But this new adventure, with its long-term opportunity to create whole worlds for the entertainment-starved Primordials – while simultaneously protecting heaven and Earth – well, Bacchus was, as he put it, the most happy of grand illusionists.

"You are perfect for this," Tamara told him, grabbing his hand and squeezing with affection.

"He'll have an outlet, at least," Cupid muttered, loud enough for at least a few of us to hear.

"We should go," I said, disrupting this moment of lighthearted rest which we all needed so badly. It was a shame, but it had to be done. "We have unfinished business."

Chapter 28

DO'S

"Places, everyone! Plaaaaaces!" Bacchus sang in a high pitch, waving a white lace handkerchief in the air that perfectly matched the flaring lace at the wrist of his blouse. "Pleeeease take your seats, ladies, gentlemen, and everyone in betweeeeen."

The largest congregation of Celestials ever seen outside Olympus, possibly anywhere, deposited their empty glasses of white wine atop the nearest column tabletop and hustled to claim a seat. I chose to stand beside the chairs along the groom's side, although that distinction wasn't being made here. My chosen spot gave me a good view of the curving eastern edge of this newly formed island floating in the South Pacific.

The weather was perfect. The late afternoon sunlight carried a golden glow quite unusual for this time of day. Apollo saw to that. The heavenly chorus, dressed in white, that had been charming the chatting guests with their sweet harmonies, allowed their final, lingering note to be swept away by the island breeze. Their accompanying orchestra played white-gold instruments and followed with their own last note. The atmosphere was both soothing and charged.

An almost imperceptible whisper of water breaking

at the surface drew my eyes toward the vast Pacific to my right. Heads and torsos rose from the waters, countless in number. I wondered if the entire population of marine gods and merfolk was here. They were quiet and still. Only the incoming waves rolling off their back and lapping the shore made a sound. Their presence made me summon driftwood from throughout the Pacific. We'd need it later.

Stragglers on land took their seats in lovely, beckoning chairs made of white wood with curved backs and draped with the most delicate, light pink fabric, translucent of course. The fabric was fastened with white ribbon and tied around dusty rose bouquets.

I discovered I didn't need to stand. Bacchus solved the problem of seated guests' having to crane their necks back to see the wedding party arrive. He enchanted the chairs, as only the best wedding planner could, so that, as guests sat, their chair rose a few centimeters off the ground and swiveled for easy viewing.

I scanned the crowd. All of Olympus was here. So were the gods and immortals who lived elsewhere. Everyone had been invited. Bacchus told me that Venus volunteered to write and send each and every wedding invitation. They too were gorgeous, of course, featuring rolling, gold cursive on white cardstock with pink flourishes at the corners that were both embossed and foil-stamped. The invitations were then perfumed, wrapped just once with cream-colored, gold-flecked lace, and sealed with golden wax. Importantly, thanks to the whole apple-to-the-fairest-Trojan-War fiasco, Venus decided not to exclude anyone.

Bacchus told me in confidence that he prepared for the worst actors by preparing them extra special wine spiked with a happiness potion. All guests were given their wine as they entered and signed the guestbook, of which Cornelius was in charge as official record keeper.

I spotted Vulcan seated next to Venus in the front row, nearest the sand. She was wearing an oversized, ill-fitting beige flop of a dress. How kind of her. The attempt at frumpiness still hadn't stopped Mars from sitting next to her, though. That would be trouble.

A quick scan of seats led my eyes to fall on Pluto, the only being there dressed in black and clearly smoldering at having to be here. Proserpina had a hand on him, preventing his escape. She wore a high-necked, sunshine yellow dress with matching sash and wide-brimmed hat. It was tasteful and quite becoming against her now-rosy skin. Pluto had a matching yellow boutonnière smashed against his robes. The flowers' petals were blackening. I was sure they'd disintegrate before the vows.

Mercury was there, hovering around Jupiter until the king took a seat in the front row. Mercury sat a few rows back. I imagine he was there to suck up. We gods do need to make up sooner or later as we've got to live with each other for eternity.

I stilled my hands – they were surprisingly shaky

– and looked beyond the chairs, west, toward the enormous white tent. Just looking at it soothed me. It was made of white lilies with creamy pink centers, connected who knows how. I imagine Bacchus used white vines or maybe bleached twine or possibly just hopes and dreams to hold it all together. However he'd managed it, the tent, the whole affair was beautiful.

A slotted drape in the tent separated to reveal a previously hidden member of the orchestra, who stepped out. He was an incredibly good-looking love angel. If I weren't a chaste goddess, if I didn't know just how much trouble romantic entanglements could bring, I would have definitely been interested. But I knew I was just getting swept up in the moment, drunk with the romance all around me. It really was lovely.

The hunk brought a white-gold herald trumpet to his lips and blew a series of fine, regal notes to announce the start of nuptials. He stepped aside, and the quieted orchestra commenced anew, led by Apollo, conducting.

I looked back from my brother to the tent and was happily surprised to see three flower girls – young ladies – who I hadn't expected to ever see again. Medusa, Stheno, and Euryale stepped out wearing flowing, floor-length dresses of blushing pink. My eyes flew to the seated guests, and I spotted Minerva with a contented smile stretched across an unusually tranquil face. My eyes caught Bacchus', who nodded with a grin of his own.

The ladies' silver baskets overflowed with white, cream, and pink flower petals, which they scattered onto the grass all the way to the arbor at the sand line where Juno stood alone, as the goddess of marriage, ready to officiate the ceremony. The girls turned and took their seats at the far end of the first row.

Another mini-serenade preceded Pip, who floated out wearing a tiny white tux and carrying two rings atop a puff of cloud set inside a clamshell. Each of the rose-gold rings sparkled with a single, large, inset diamond.

Pip drifted down the aisle, smiling like he could kiss everyone in sight. I suspected he'd spent too much time helping Cupid prepare today, of all days, when the lover's aura was probably palpable. Pip reached Juno, turned the other way, and sat.

And then a gentle, trilling note from the herald trumpet let us know the moment we'd been waiting for had come at last. The trumpeter paused for a moment before proceeding elegantly and perfectly into a new composition welcoming the bride and groom.

Cupid and Tamara stepped out as one.

I gasped along with everyone else. If there had ever been a more handsome couple, I hadn't seen them. And as I thought about that, I realized it must have truly been Cupid's love gilding them so brilliantly because surely Venus made an inspiring bride, but I couldn't even remember her special moment. These two lovers were a vision.

Guests in chairs stood to drink them in.

Cupid wore all white. His tuxedo bore peak lapels, his shirt a batwing collar, and his puff tie carried hints of soft pink splotches. His pocket square was a stronger pink, as was the single flower I'd brought for his lapel.

The flower was a new species that I cultivated myself, striking as an open lily with its long, pink, pointed petals, but its inside rows ruffled and shortened as they approached the central dome, which puffed and flamed hot pink. It was striking and what I imagined passionate love might look like.

Tamara, however, outshined even my unique flower in her white silk dress. Its straight skirt was delicately draped with barely-there pink silk threading which cascaded behind her in a lacy train. The fitted bodice had a square neckline leading into tulle cap shoulders. Her black, curled hair was stacked high and pinned by pink gems that matched those hanging off her earlobes. Finally, her bouquet tied it all in. About a foot and a half long, it was a mix of my flowers and those presented as a gift from Ceres and Proserpina. Actually, every other flower at the ceremony came from those two. A gift. And there were undoubtedly tens of thousands of flowers. I'd tipped off my neebo to the bounty to be found here.

The music changed, and the pair walked forward. They seemed to float as they approached a new future together.

Some of the guests murmured their appreciation. Other couldn't resist clapping gloved hands, even though the time wasn't right yet. Bacchus' wine no doubt. And some guests even muffled tortured sobs. I looked around to find stifled weeping coming from a gaggle of female love angels, who looked to be trying their best to contain their heartache.

I noticed Jarel standing nearby. He nudged that other Fallen Angel I'd seen at the proposal – Tommy, I believe his name was – and they slid toward the ladies.

Cupid and Tamara continued their walk up the aisle smiling at their guests until they reached Juno, who raised her arms, then lowered them to indicate guests could be seated. Juno then stepped to the right and turned back toward the left so that she was looking down the beach rather than down the aisle. The happy couple pivoted to face her straight on.

Classy. I smiled at the move. Now, no guests, by land or sea, had the couple's back to them. No guests had Juno's back blocking their view. Both groups got side views of bride, groom, and officiant.

"Friends, family, and loved ones," began Juno, raising her palms to the sky, "welcome one and all." She didn't read off a script. I imagine she's married off countless couples. "We share in the commitment between Cupid and Tamara. They ask for our support and blessings as they exchange vows."

She nodded at Cupid and stepped back.

Cupid lifted Tamara's hand, guided her forward, and then turned her around to face him. He kissed her hand before starting his vows. "Tamara, the very day I met you, you challenged me. You called me a traitor to love."

A few attendees gasped. Cupid held up a hand. Tamara curled her upper lip past her lower, stifling a giggle at the memory.

"And you weren't wrong. You knew better than I did that friendship and loyalty show love as strongly as any physical intimacy," – he brushed the back of his hand against her cheek – "any sweet act of tenderness."

Sobs broke a bit louder from the rejected angelettes in the audience. I saw Jarel and Tommy wrap consoling arms around their shoulders.

"Tamara, my darling, ma chérie, on that very first day, you talked back to me because you wouldn't let the name Cupid turn you to mush. There'd never be any groveling from you, no begging for my affections, although you yourself share kindness freely. You showed me that very day, when you traveled to The Underworld, the true face of bravery."

Several faces in the crowd turned toward each other. Apparently they didn't know that she'd taken on that dangerous mission when she and Cupid were still near strangers. Many more guests looked at Pluto, who seemed oblivious to the proceedings before him. He was staring into the sky with his mouth hanging open. Oof! I wondered how much potion Bacchus put in his drink. Maybe it was *all* potion.

"You taught me," Cupid continued, "what fidelity looks like, risking yourself to save friends."

Many eyes sought The Fallen, who were there in force. When the angelettes who had Jarel and Tommy's arms draped around their shoulders saw so many eyes upon them, the ladies clutched the lapels of their new beaus and cozied up.

"You were and are strong," Cupid said, "and you bring me a joy I've never known before.

"Tamara, I want to bring you that same kind of joy for the rest of eternity. Marriage is a partnership of love and devotion. As I've already felt that for you since day one, let's take ourselves off the market and make googly eyes only at each other, forever."

A relieved chuckle rippled across the crowd. Venus dabbed a tear. Both Mars and Vulcan whipped out their pocket squares with a snap and offered them. I hoped we'd make it through the ceremony before trouble broke. As if Venus sensed it, too, she took both squares and put a hand on the knee of each attendant. That settled them.

It was time for Tamara's vows.

"Cupid, I remember the first time you kissed me. It was to prove who you were."

Cupid tugged at his collar in mock shame.

"The second time was to shore me up. And it was that kiss that captured me." Tamara squeezed his hand. "You've been giving me your heart and soul ever since, through quiet times and remarkable adventures. You've made me a part of your life. You've made me a part of your family. You've made me yours, and you mine, forever.

"Sweetheart, I pledge my heart to you and promise to love you through anything and everything fate throws our way."

I chanced a glance at The Fates. They were hovering behind the final rows of seats, appearing as three middle-aged women in pastels. Something about them, though, gave them away. *Ah, there it is,* I thought. They had string woven through their fingers. *Yes, I suppose they can't leave their threads of life at home.*

A flutter of wings brought my attention to the front once more. Pip flitted up with the rings to hover beside Cupid. Juno stood beside Tamara. She asked her grandson, "Cupid, do you take Tamara to be your wife, to love and cherish for all eternity?"

"I do," he answered, to a not-quiet wail of tears from the back.

Mars chuckled in the front row.

Cupid took one of the rings off the cloud-pillow and placed it on Tamara's finger. "A sign of my never-ending love," he said.

Pip shifted to stand beside Tamara. Juno moved

to Cupid's side and asked her soon-to-be grand-daughter-in-law, "Tamara, do you take Cupid to be your husband, to love and cherish for all time?"

She petted his hand once before saying, "Yes, absolutely I do."

She took a ring and placed it on Cupid's finger. "My never-ending love," she said.

Juno raised her hands to the sky. I heard a collective intake of breath. "I now pronounce you husband and wife."

Cupid broke the space between them and put a hand on Tamara's shoulder before trailing it up behind her neck to cradle her head. She lifted her hands slowly. Cupid leaned in and barely touched her lips with his. He kissed her once, gently. It was such a quiet moment, so almost not-there that I wondered if I'd missed it. But when she put one hand on his shoulder, he dragged her in. He wrapped her waist with his other arm and pressed his lips against hers with a contained passion that, really, made me blush. She kissed him back, and he her, until he pressed her into a dip that left the crowd cheering.

The ocean behind them exploded in dancing water, shooting sprays that touched the sky. The merfolk splashed and clicked in their watery way. Neptune rose above the surface behind them on a coral throne and waved his golden trident. Tall waves appeared and ran parallel to the island's shore rather than toward it, like cardboard cutouts at a children's theater. Within them raced scores of the most beautiful fish I'd ever seen, some I'd never seen. The waves kept on, and I realized they'd be there throughout, a tribute to Tamara, the animal lover of the pair.

The newly married couple turned to face their adoring audience and waved like the superstar celebrity couple they were destined to become. Their public cheered and whistled. Even Pluto brought his bony hands together, although I got the sense he was imitating the blur of people around him. Still, maybe the good vibes would keep for a few days. Maybe The Underworld would be made more bearable for a bit.

Cupid and Tamara strode down the aisle in easy spirits.

The structured part of the ceremony, done, I thought. *Now the reception. Oh my, I wonder what's in store. The gods do love a good party.*

Chapter 29

DON'T'S

I dropped my third glass of wine onto a columned table-top and marveled at how wonderful the day was going. All around, people mingled and chatted and danced. The driftwood I'd summoned arrived over dinner. I had it rip itself into planks and lain out to make a long pier extending far into the water. That way land guests could mingle and dance with marine guests. I wondered if any new romance might come of it.

Looking back at the land festivities, I spotted The Fates at the gift table, shaking boxes. I sauntered over to hear them guessing what was inside and handing it to a sister, who inevitably guessed something different, as did the third. I had a sneaking suspicion someone hexed the table to prevent even seers from peeking.

The dinner had been delicious. Jupiter's chefs were restored by the Jani, thank time itself, and they'd prepared an enormous bounty of ambrosia fit for an entire king-dom. The cooks debuted mouthwatering new flavors that they'd even whipped into intricate shapes, like peacocks and corals and shooting stars. The cake was the supreme work of art, though. It looked like a jumble of multi-col-ored wedding-gift boxes netted in striped red ribbon. The gifts were each a sumptuous dessert, and the ribbon was pulled sugar. But it was the miniature bride and groom atop the whole thing that caught everyone's imagination. They were exact, though mini, figures of Cupid and Tamara, animated to rotate through a small series of actions. One second they were drawing the bow, the next high-fiving, and they ended finally kissing in congratulations.

The dinner tables were whisked away for the reception. Cupid and Tamara led first dance as a married couple: a waltz conducted by Apollo's orchestra. The bride and groom defined elegance with their straight posture, sweeping steps, and perfect execution. After, they bowed and let others onto the floor. I knew, before long, night would come, and the dancing would become decidedly freer.

I was going to compliment Bacchus on his amazing job as event organizer when I spotted him tending bar. I laughed, so perfectly did he look the part. He'd spiked his hair and donned a white dress shirt, black vest, and black bow tie. He was drying a glass with a dishtowel while prattling with a guest. I got the impression he was sharing a long story. I almost envied his lightheartedness.

A tap on my shoulder turned me around. There stood Cupid with his hand extended. "May I have this dance?" he asked.

I was not so out of touch to realize that many women and goddesses would commit crimes for the chance to dance with Cupid, but they had hopes and intentions which I did not. "I'm honored," I answered. And I was.

A few steps convinced me of his mastery at leading. I allowed myself to enjoy his guidance while looking into his eyes. "I'm happy for you, Cupid."

"Thanks," he said, swinging me under his extended arm and bringing me back into our step rhythm. "For everything."

"I heard you had a visit from The Fates since we were in The Underworld."

Cupid didn't break his step pattern. "A lot's happened in the past month. They came to my house, and I took them into the parlor overlooking the pond. I thought they might like the view. I forgot that that's where I keep all their unread scrolls. They handed me a fresh one that said, 'The world needs you more than Council does.'"

"Mmmm," I said.

"I'd already decided to keep doing my thing," he said. "I told them – nicely – that if they'd given me such clear advice before, maybe I'd have known what to do. Morta walked over to the shelves and pulled out three scrolls, which of course made all the rest spill across the floor. The first she handed me was a mess of cryptic poetry, something about 'a hiss of night.' Honestly, if I'd have read it, I'd have thought they were talking about farts."

I looked away to not laugh.

"The second at least had the word 'snake' in it along with 'sky,' but if I'd have read it, I'd've thought it warned of a storm picking up snakes in an updraft. The third was a lot clearer. It said, 'Medusa will attack.' I should have read the scrolls."

I kept my mouth shut.

"I think Medusa chose her moment for revenge because there was going to be an official announcement of succession," Cupid said. He looked over my shoulder a moment before meeting my eyes again, and I had the curious sensation that he was confiding in me. "It wasn't just about revenge, was it, Diana? Tamara thinks it was a chance for her to show Council that women need to be better treated in the new regime."

"Tamara now has the protection that many females do not," I said. "You can influence change."

Cupid looked over at his bride, who was dancing with Cornelius. The Celestial wore a grey suit and had greased his puffy red hair in an effort to tame it. He looked dapper.

"I don't intend to retire to Council," Cupid warned. "I'll stick with my lovifying duties, but I see her point and yours. We need progress."

I nodded.

"Tamara asked me why I didn't control the water in Horror's armor to move him."

"And why didn't you?" I prompted.

"Because that would make me a tyrant," Cupid answered. "I mean, prison is the most compassionate place for the Primordials, but, for everyone else, I'd rather not go down the path of taking away their free will," Cupid answered.

Cupid twirled me under his arm again, only this time brought me back with a bit of a snap. "Is it the same for you?"

I raised a brow but kept step.

"The Fates told me you're much more powerful than anyone knows, that I was wise to seek an alliance."

I wasn't about to reveal my secret to anyone, especially now that the neebo had infiltrated the mind of everyone here, including the merfolk, thanks to my suggestion to Minerva that those out at sea should enjoy the flowers, too. Minerva scooped up armfuls to dump into the water. I saw plenty of green arms reach out for them.

I had no intention of robbing people their choices. But, just as Cupid had to move the Primordials to a better place, I have to see the present from more than one angle.

"I have no designs on free will," I said.

Someone stumbled into me, and I turned to see my brother with Bacchus' perpetually refilling wine goblet.

"You there!" he said, pointing one of the fingers around the goblet at Cupid. "I jes' realized some'n. If you can control water, you could control those arrows during our shootin' match a few hundred years ago! Maybe you didn' win our match fair 'n square!"

I looked to Cupid, who shrugged his shoulders.

"So I still say I'm the best shooter ever!" Apollo

said and hiccuped. He waited for a rebuttal and, when he didn't get one, stumbled off toward the ocean and a pack of mermaids dancing in a group. I sincerely hoped he'd fall into the water and make a fool of himself.

"Jarel's got the job permanently," Cupid said to no particular prompting from me. "He'll guard the CC starting tomorrow. Vulcan's robots are guarding Olympus tonight."

"As are my griffin and my … other helpers."

Cupid raised a brow but simply answered, "Glad to hear it." He put one hand on my back to lead me through a promenade step before saying, "Jupiter cleaned up Earth, and Juno's memory trick worked so mortals don't remember anything."

"Makes our jobs easier if we're not despised," I said, wondering how closely memory aligns with free will.

"Did you hear how Minerva and Neptune were punished?" Cupid asked me. I did indeed hear, right from the king and queen as they were formulating the ideas. I might have swayed them.

"Neptune's been saddled with a chastity belt for the next 500 years," Cupid said. He waited for me to look surprised, so I feigned shock.

"Vulcan made it on royal order, although I hear he thought loads of gods could use one. Anyway, it's skintight and matches his scales. Neat idea. It's a deprivation that won't kill him and can't trigger righteous indignation on his part. I guess that was important here, that the punishment wouldn't be so cruel as to incite later revenge."

I thought that was a wise caveat. That's why I telepathed it.

"And Minerva's been fitted with false eyelashes. Non-removable. She'll have to wear those for the next hundred years."

"Oh?" I asked, raising an eyebrow. "I do hear they're rather uncomfortable."

Cupid twirled me once more while laughing. He knew I wasn't so out of touch.

"The thinking with Minerva is that she failed to see a disciple's anguish and then failed to see how much her curse harmed her, so Vulcan's lashes keep her eyes open – not endlessly for the next hundred years but enough to disrupt her sleep and life. Enough to remind her that people need to be *seen.*"

I looked toward the sea hoping to catch a glimpse of either malefactor's new fashion wear, but Bacchus sideswiped us as he hustled past with drinks in hand. It occurred to me that he was awfully involved in the work behind this wedding, but some people do love hosting. Cupid and I followed him with our eyes to see where he was going in such a rush.

He was headed toward Mars and Vulcan, who were chest-to-chest at the deejay table. Habandash was getting ready to take over the music responsibilities from

Apollo's orchestra, which was playing just as well without their conductor as they had with him.

The rivals for Venus' hand were nearly to blows.

"Awww, now, come on, fellas," slushed a slow voice from nearby. The crowd parted to make way for its owner. Pluto stopped beside the gods and rested a hand on each of their shoulders. They flinched from the likely-dreadful contact. "We're at a paaaaarty," Pluto said with a voice that dripped like molasses. "This is a haaaappy occasion. Let's have a gooood time." He snagged the drinks Bacchus offered and handed them to Venus' flames before snagging one for himself from a bystander. "Here's to the happy couple!"

"The happy couple!" sang a hundred voices.

Pluto stared wobbly at Mars and Vulcan until the discomfort made them drink. A few seconds later, their shoulders relaxed and they went their separate ways. Luckily, neither was headed toward Venus, who had ditched her shabby attire from earlier and now wore a skin-tight, glittering, pink lace gown, looking absolutely like a 1940s Hollywood star.

Bacchus came back around and must have seen an opportunity where others did not. He stopped at the gift table and asked Decima, the apportioner fate, to dance. I looked at Cupid.

"I think everyone else is afraid to get near them," Cupid said. "They might get caught up in a prophecy."

"Ah, but Bacchus would love that," I replied. "Or at least being supplied with prophecies."

"The Fates are next on my dance card," Cupid said. "Wish me luck."

"Oh! Cupid?" I said after he walked me off the dance floor. He raised his bushy eyebrows in question. I tapped his new wedding ring. "You be sure to keep that on your finger."

He laughed, and I knew he thought I was reminding him to be faithful. But I happened to know that Vulcan forged those rings himself because he wanted to give Tamara something he wished he'd have had when he married the goddess of love.

"Da rings be trackin' devices," I heard him whisper in Tamara's ear. I scanned the crowd and found him dancing with the bride – well, shuffling is more like it, as you'd expect an underground god to move. "Might come in handy when ya marryin' an immortal who's hankerin' is love. No need ta tell 'im. Bes' to keep it yer li'l secret." He winked at her.

Tamara looked past him and caught me laughing. I decided to rescue her. When I tapped Vulcan's shoulder, he scowled but relinquished the bride. I performed a little side-to-side step to the fast beat. Tamara joined in, a few feet in front of me. Venus sauntered up, too, and soon we formed a circle of women on the dance floor. Within minutes, the circle grew. Ladies off the dance floor ran on to join in. Deejay Habandash mixed in a song with lyrics about lovely ladies. The men watched appreciatively.

We were having a ball, laughing and sweating, and Habandash was spinning records really well until we heard a needle scratch, at which point the music slowed. I doubted it was by the deejay's choice, but before I could protest, I was in Mars' arms, and he was sweeping me away to another part of the dance floor.

Normally I'd have fought such masculine liberties, but, well, evening was dawning, and the night was young.

Tyrone drew Cupid's shiny red limousine to a lighted spot near the twinkling dance floor. Twilight was upon us. Before we knew it, cherubs were showering the bride and groom with baby's breath. In a moment, they'd run off to an undisclosed location for their honeymoon. Although everyone asked, all day, where they'd be vacationing, neither Cupid nor Tamara would tell a soul. They didn't want to be disturbed. I couldn't blame them. I still felt bad for my interruption at the waterfall.

When Tyrone stepped out of the limo, I saw him run up to the same angelette who'd been fighting at his side in Moscow, a short, big-bottomed Celestial standing under a string of lights. He seemed to be talking quickly.

He pointed at her and then the limo. She put a hand to her chest. "Me?" I imagined her saying.

As I watched, two arrows zipped out of the darkness between us and struck each of them right in the heart. I spun around to see from whence they came and found Cupid and Tamara in post-strike pose. *Gods,* what a vision they made: bride and groom in power pose, dressed in bright white formals, being showered by baby's breath, at one of the most exquisite moments in their life.

The crowd erupted. Glasses clinked all around. Merfolk tails thundered against the water. Cupid and Tamara hugged. And when I looked back at the love angels that had been their target, I witnessed how the feelings they clearly had for one another revealed themselves. Tyrone stooped down for a kiss, and she met him on tiptoe. I clutched my heart.

The crowd surged forward, and I watched as Cupid and Tamara got into the limo, escaping to a new life together.

As I waved goodbye, someone bumped my shoulder. I looked down to see Venus at my side and her usual surrounding gaggle of Celestial men. She hugged me, which she'd never done before. I felt … blessed.

She said,

> "How right the world e'er love shines through,
> when sweet, young lovers bid adieu
> to fear, mistrust, and ballyhoo

and rather choose to rendezvous

with they who hath a heart that's true."

She dabbed a tear with a pink handkerchief she pulled from her cleavage. Then she waved goodbye with it as Cupid's limo faded into the darkness. I waved, too, and contemplated.

I didn't have as much experience with love as Venus did, but I did know one thing. If a god can control anything and anyone, yet that god chooses to relinquish control, chooses to let people govern themselves and simply *be* themselves, that god is showing more love than anyone I'd ever known. Cupid understood love better than I'd ever given him credit for.

Jupiter was right. Cupid is the strongest god. Cupid is the god of love.

Who's Who in Order of Reference

Diana – Roman goddess of the hunt. Seer. Savior and hero to the neebo.

Cupid – God of love. Son to Venus and Mars. Once dethroned but now two-time hero of Olympus.

Tamara *(pronounced TAM ruh)* – Cupid's main squeeze. Once a member of The Fallen love angels but now two-time heroine of Olympus. Brave adventurer who once trespassed in The Underworld and stole the allegiance of Pluto's hellhound. She now lives in Pluto's crosshairs.

Stag – Diana's companion in her native woodlands. Also a warning of how mistreatment toward her might end (see Actaeon).

Actaeon *(pronounced ACK tee on)* – Foolish mortal who dared spy on Diana's bathing. She transformed him into a stag, and he was promptly torn apart by his own hunting dogs.

Celestials – All those immortals who reside in or are part of the divine kingdom of Olympus.

Apollo – God of the sun, healing, and music. Son and watchman to Jupiter.

Pluto – God of The Underworld and ruler of the dead. Brother to Jupiter and Neptune. Henpecked husband of Proserpina.

Cerberus – Three-headed hellhound and former guardian of the entrance to The Underworld. Current guard dog of Cupid Castle, its inhabitants, and its resident koi fish. Carnivore.

Bacchus *(pronounced BAH kus)* – God of theatre, wine, and merrymaking. Troublemaker. Hedonist. Optimist. Son to Jupiter.

Panthers – Bacchus' troupe of three black panthers. The fierce felines pull his chariot and serve as his guardians and helpers.

Jupiter – God of the sky and thunder, king of the gods, husband to (and brother of) Juno. Brother to Neptune and Pluto. Prodigious philanderer. Father to thousands. Weapon of choice: thunderbolt.

Neptune – Roman god of the seas. Brother to Jupiter and Pluto. God whose sexual relations with Diana's disciple Medusa incited the goddess' curse.

Cornelius – Once a member of The Fallen. Now Scribe of Olympus and Assistant to Habandash. Official record keeper. In charge of Cupid's daily lovifying Hit List.

Tommy – Once a member of The Fallen and Tamara's most devout defender. Now provides the few Still Fallen with opportunities to regain Heaven's Goodwill.

Tyrone – Former chauffeur, personal assistant, and spy to Cupid. Now prolific love angel. Crushing on a lady friend.

Pip – Jupiter's cherubic messenger. Was instrumental in Cupid's dethronement. Now instrumental in Cupid's adventures. Talkative but colorful.

Jarel *(pronounced juh REL)* – Once a member of The Fallen. Later, butler to Cupid. Now bored apprentice to Mars.

Vulcan – God of volcanoes, lava, fire, and metalworking. Son to Jupiter and Juno. Husband to (and constant pursuer of) Venus. Brother to Mars, Venus' paramour. Tool-maker. Inventor. Genius.

Neebo – Microscopic, transparent, and winged creatures that inhabit the brains of hosts to share that being's perceptions with Diana.

Griffin [Nightfall, Ember, Snowlight] – Ancient creatures, their front halves that of an eagle, their back halves that of a lion. Hunted by immortals. Denied by mortals.

The Jani [Janus & Janice] – God/dess of beginnings & endings, past & future. Two god/desses in one body, sharing one head, their faces pointing in opposite directions. Guardians of Council Colossus, the celestial city hall.

Habandash – Jupiter's personal assistant charged with overseeing Olympic and Earthly affairs. Once deposed Cupid and instated a fraud in his place. Later re-established Cupid as Olympus' lead lover.

Venus – Goddess of love, beauty, and sexuality. Married to Vulcan, yet is a frequent paramour of Vulcan's brother, Mars, with whom she bore Cupid. Poet. Wise counselor. Dangerously distracting.

Mercury – God of commerce, journeys, and trickery. Guide of the newly deceased to The Underworld. Son to Jupiter and deliverer of royal messages before his attempted coup. Currently exiled.

Minerva – Goddess of wisdom, crafts, and strategy in war. Wears armor weaved from her father's tendons and cartilage. Cursed Medusa and her sisters (below) for in-temple acts with Neptune, turning them into Gorgons.

Mars – God of war, father to Cupid, and the most prominent "other man" in Venus' life. Brother to Venus' husband, Vulcan, thus constantly earning side-eye. Harbors no fear of snakes or anything else.

Eris *(pronounced AIR ees)* – Goddess of Discord. Uninvited guest who disrupted a wedding by offering a golden apple inscribed "To the fairest." Arguably the true instigator of the Trojan War.

Juno – Goddess of the state and marriage, queen of the gods, and sister/wife to Jupiter. Mother to Mars (via sheer will) and grandmother to Cupid. Detector and punisher of Jupiter's mistresses. Killjoy of shenanigans.

Paris – Mortal youth trusted by Jupiter to fairly decide ownership of a controversial apple. His decision, a/k/a the Judgment of Troy, sparked the Trojan War.

Troy – Setting of the decade-long Trojan War between Mycenaean Greeks and Trojans, sparked by Paris' abduction of Helen, to whom he felt entitled as the reward for his Judgment.

Helen – Wife of Menelaus of Sparta. Abducted by Paris and taken to Troy. A decade of fighting ensues to get her back.

Ceres *(pronounced SEH rees)* – Goddess of the harvest, grains, and growth. Mother to Proserpina.

Primordials (Horror, Rage, and others) – Oldest and wildest gods, chaotic in form and attributes. Ruthless. Untamable. Ancestors to the Titans and later Olympians. Now imprisoned in Tartarus, below The Underworld.

Nyx – Primordial goddess, nighttime personified.

Titans – Descendants of the Primordials and barbaric ancestors to the Olympians. Now imprisoned in Tartarus, below The Underworld.

Prometheus – Titan who defied Jupiter by stealing fire and giving it to mortals. Now imprisoned in Tartarus, punished by having his liver eaten every day and regenerated every night.

The Fates [Nona, Decima, and Morta] – Goddesses of destiny and measurers of lifespans. Seers. Frequently speak in riddles.

Gorgons [Medusa, Stheno, and Euryale] – Mortal sisters so cursed by Minerva that all who see them turn to stone. Most known for their hair of living, venomous snakes and their horrifying visages. Their scaled torsos maintain a human form to the waist, where their snake tails take over, ending with terror-inducing rattles.

Medusa *(pronounced meh DOO suh)* – Most famous Gorgon. Her sexual encounter with Neptune at Minerva's temple offended the goddess, who cursed her and her sisters Stheno and Euryale.

Pegasus – Winged horse that is the result of Neptune's copulation with Medusa. Supposedly sprung from Medusa's body after her beheading.

Nona *(pronounced NO nuh)* – One of three Fates. Spins a mortal's thread of life.

Decima *(pronounced DEH sih muh)* – One of three Fates. Measures a mortal's thread of life.

Morta – One of three Fates. Cuts a mortal's thread of life, making her the most feared.

Perseus – Demigod son of Zeus. Famous as the slayer of Medusa.

Minerva's owls (small and large) – Minerva's companions, helpers, and transport.

Shakespeare – English poet and playwright. Widely regarded as the best dramatist in history. Known as The Bard. Regularly quoted by Bacchus.

Mars' wolves – Found on reliefs in Mars' chariot and able to animate at will. Mars' companions and occasional transport.

Proserpina – Goddess of The Underworld. Wife to Pluto. Daughter to Ceres. Her return to sunshine every spring and summer makes the Earth burst forth in vegetation.

Jupiter's chefs – Culinary artists in charge of creating the divine ambrosia needed to keep Celestials immortal.

Gorgons' Followers – Mortals loyal to the Gorgons who oftentimes blind themselves to better serve their mistresses.

Rage – Primordial escapee of The Underworld. Chaotic being of smoke armored in fire.

Horror – Primordial escapee of The Underworld. Chaotic being armored in crushed debris.

Stheno *(pronounced ss THEN oh)* – Gorgon discernable for her red hairsnakes. Faithful sister to Medusa.

Euryale *(pronounced yoo RYE uh lee)* – Gorgon discernable for her grey body and clawed, brass gloves. Faithful sister to Medusa.

Kraken – Neptune's tentacled, giant sea monster. Called by many names over the centuries, including Leviathan and Hellmouth. Often mistaken for giant sea squid and even whales.

Tyrone's lady friend – Tyrone's dance partner after Cupid's defeat of Mercury. Ally in the fight against Horror. Crushing on Tyrone.

Merfolk – Neptune's people. Guardians of and populators of the seas. Fierce when need be. Friendly whenever able. Much like the rest of us.

Angelettes *(pronounced AIN jel ETS)* – Those particular lady love angels who were once Cupid's groupies and now seek validation from other males who will no doubt tire eventually of ladies who can't stand on their own.

Q&A with the Author

Cupid's been on many fun adventures. How do you feel wrapping up his story?

I'm thrilled for Cupid and even a bit proud of myself. Cupid's had a great many ups and downs in this trilogy and he's been very challenged, but he's grown as a character and become a better person. In *God Awful Loser*, Cupid was certainly not the most likable character I've ever read.

He had a lot to learn about treating people with respect. His privileged life, his skewed way of valuing people, and his wild celebrity were the origins of who he was. He needed to be taken out of his comfort zone, as so many of us do, in order to stretch himself and see how much better he could become. Throughout *God Awful Loser*, into *God Awful Thief*, and during every bit of *God Awful Rebel*, Cupid transforms. He learns what love really looks like. By the end of the series, he's a changed god and one that I think most people would be glad to call a friend. Cupid's also taken *me* on an adventure. The picture opposite is me in Paris before the iconic Eiffel Tower and pointing to its duplicate on the cover of *God Awful Loser*. What a ride it's been! What a happily ever after.

God Awful Rebel introduces us to many new characters. How do you come up with their wonderful quirks?

Some of the new characters are gods or goddesses long established in Roman mythology. Interestingly, though, the gods tend to have multiple – even conflicting – domains, so I've often had to choose which part of their personality to highlight. Once I did that, I let my creativity soar. For example, I imagined what might trigger the goddess of marriage into reacting during a certain scene, and I wrote to that. For some gods, I made up powers that I felt would help them control their territory.

When I create characters who weren't gods, that's when I could really let my imagination rip. The neebo were great fun to write. Imagining what they'd look like to be able to snuggle up into the cranny of a brain, ha! I wrote what I pictured, and was immensely pleased by the outcome.

I'm often asked how I come up with story lines and character traits. What I most often say is that the act of creating makes you more creative. What I mean is that regular writing keeps your mind on your story well after you've abandoned the keyboard for the day. When the story is marinating in your mind for perhaps years, you will naturally come up with funny and insightful moments or twists of plot. I hope you enjoy reading them as much as I enjoyed creating them.

Whoa, what's with this art?

Way back before *God Awful Loser* was published, my husband decided to have a little fun and draw a few of the characters. Jeff (Miracola) is a professional illustrator who's worked on many big name properties, and he's known for his fantasy paintings and complex ink drawings. For Loser, he created simplified line drawings of Cupid, Venus, Pluto, and Mars. We decided to include his drawings here as thanks to you readers who stuck through to the end of the series. You'll notice that Venus isn't just one woman.

If you've read the series, you'll know why.

If you've drawn any of the characters in my books, please do take a picture and send it my way. I love hearing from readers!

Is hearing from and meeting readers a fun part of your writing life?

Absolutely. Let me say it again. I love hearing from readers, and not just readers of my own books. Widely read people are great conversationalists. If they've also read my

book, they'll share their thoughts on it, provide fascinating observations, and ask genuinely thought-provoking questions. Whether I'm speaking at a conference, signing at a bookstore, or chatting as the guest author at a book club, I'm enjoying myself.

Who's your favorite Roman god?

Oof, tough question. I once answered this Venus because she was kind to her admirers in a way Cupid wasn't. I still love to write Venus because she wields a sharp tongue and speaks in verse, but I have to say that Bacchus has turned out to be an amazing character. He is so passionate about life and so honest in who he is that you just can't help but like him. At least I can't. And Tamara is a gem. So brave. So resourceful. She's the smart, strong woman I'd hoped to write one day.

Then how could you have done to her what you did?

Oh, I knew some people would be mad at me for that. Okay, a disclaimer: If you haven't read *God Awful Rebel* in its entirety yet, skip to the next question because this answer contains spoilers. No, seriously, look away. You're still here? Okay, don't say I didn't warn you.

The easy answer is that *I* didn't turn Tamara to stone. *She*

did by being so caring that she chose to protect Diana before protecting herself. Why you'd pin her actions on me, the writer, is beyond me, but, fine, if you're going to make me answer for her actions, let's just say that her actions are in keeping with her character, forcing Cupid's actions to also be in keeping with his newer, transformed character. Cupid is the god of love, so he will act on that love and

be motivated to save her. In so doing, he saves everyone.

What's the meaning of the flowers in Diana's Neebo Bouquet?

The flowers Diana chose visualize Medusa's journey. Snap-dragons represent presumption and deception. Medusa was presumed to be guilty of a crime and deceived by the goddess she worshiped, who really should have given her the benefit of any doubt. Monkshood means beware because a deadly foe is near. Poppies represent eternal sleep or oblivion, caused by her curse. Pigeonwings represent womanhood, what Medusa once was, what she always was inside, and the hope of what she would be again.

How do you plan a story arc that goes over three books?

In the Q&A with the Author at the end of *God Awful Loser*, I said that I was better at outlining as a child than I was as an adult. That's how it was for that particular book. I've since embraced outlining, and I think probably most series writers have to do that if they hope to truly close out character arcs and wrap up subplots to satisfaction. Making an outline and setting out notes before you even start the actual writing sounds an awful lot like homework – and it is – but it's still a lot of fun, and I'm convinced it's the best way to write long stories that connect as a whole.

Did you always want to be a writer?

No and yes. No in that, as a child, I never really aspired to being an author like those writers whose books I read so voraciously during many happy afternoons in the library. I thought of authors as somewhat brilliant. To be able to weave together an interesting story and make me feel what the author felt across space and time by words on a page? Magic.

But yes in that, as a college student, I chose to become a writer and studied journalism. By graduation, I'd written for newspapers, TV, and radio. And in the decades that followed, I became a full-fledged professional journalist. I wrote a great deal of news copy, so I was certainly a writer.

However, it wasn't until the early 2000s that I decided to dabble in fiction during my off hours. And that brought me back to my childhood memories. Now that I had so much writing experience, I did indeed want to be a writer – of fiction as well as nonfiction.

Looking back at my life (which is the only way one can see it, obviously), I realize that I was constantly reading and/or writing from the first days I was able. I can't imagine a better way to spend my time and energies.

What's the most surprising thing you learned writing this series?

That I was far more creative than I'd ever imagined. As I said previously, I spent my career writing news stories, that is, nonfiction. As such, I didn't have much reason for confidence when it came to writing fiction, but I knew that I'd get better at it the more I did it. My first few novels were anemic, but the more I worked, the better they got and the more creative I became. I still have moments of struggle, but they are fewer and seem less insurmountable. And I'm sometimes caught off guard by my creative moments. I often laugh as I see what I typed and ask myself, Where did that come from? Those are great moments.

Do you feel lonely being a writer?

Not at all. I'm very comfortable being in my own company. I enjoy solitude (which is not the same thing as loneliness) and am happy listening to my own thoughts as I formulate ideas and stories. I imagine that if you dislike being alone and keeping still for sustained amounts of time, you would have trouble settling yourself to write a book. Having said that, I'm also a social and active person, so I find time in my life for both. I'm lucky to have friends and family with varied interests that allow me to find my fit with all of them.

Acknowledgments

Your truest friends are those who are there for you and who encourage you in whatever worthy endeavor you want to do. I'm lucky to have those kinds of people in my life.

Thanks first and foremost to my husband, Jeff, who comes up with so many great ideas that he sometimes doesn't remember them. He later reads these marvelous bits fleshed out within my pages and is amazed by my creativity. I laugh at him a lot.

Huge thanks go out to Valerie Biel, Keith Pitsch, and Dave Emanuel, who together form an epic writers' group. I never want to let them down.

Hugs and love to my kids, Corina, Antonia, and Armando, to whom this book is dedicated, for always cheering me on. I love that they believe in me.

Finally, I want to thank you, dear reader, for allowing yourself to fall into the world of my stories. Thank you for sharing your time with me. Thanks for telling me how much you've enjoyed these adventures. Your emails and kind words at bookstores, libraries, and conferences mean the world to me.

About the Author

S ilvia Acevedo is a journalist and former television news anchor who's spent many years reporting objective fact. She's interviewed presidential candidates, covered national and international stories, and given breaking news reports for CNN and local television and radio stations around the country. Silvia guest hosted a morning talk show for a local NBC affiliate and continues to write for corporate clients. Roman gods, however, were shockingly absent in her profession, so she decided to bring fiction – especially mythology – back into her life.

Silvia deftly weaves vignettes of ancient myth into a wholly new and laugh-out-loud story for the modern age. The hunt for truth and adventure ensnares us in *God Awful Rebel*, the third and final pursuit in the *God Awful* series.

Silvia has been a member of the Society of Children's Book Writers and Illustrators for more than a decade and serves as a coordinator for her local chapter. She lives with her husband, Jeff Miracola, who is an accomplished fantasy illustrator and children's book artist, and their children just outside of Milwaukee.

Find her at www.silviaacevedo.com.

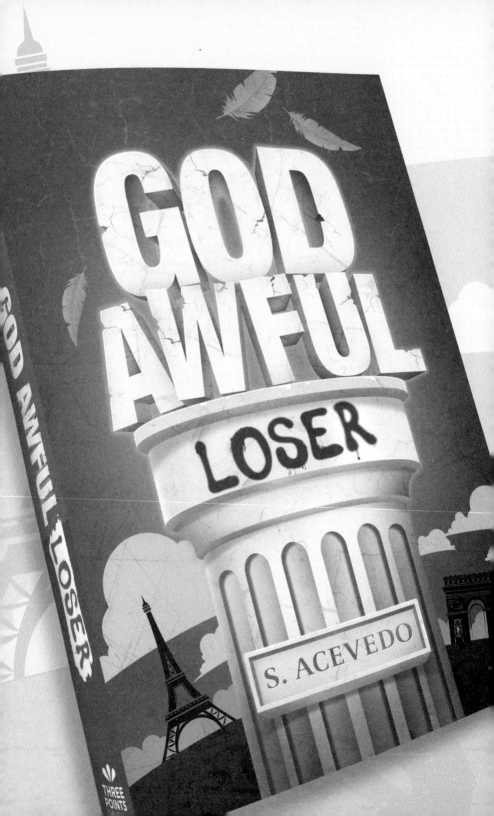

Life's good at the top.
Until you're not.

The son of the God of War has it all, and the smooth-talking, jet-setting master knows it. The once chubby cherub now has adoring fans, a shiny red limousine, and a mansion nearly, almost, not quite big enough to hold his enormous and ever-growing ego.

But everything changes for the sloppy, ill-aiming love god when a meddling stranger challenges him for his crown. Not even the advice of his war-mongering father, Mars, and embarrassingly underdressed mother, Venus, can save Cupid from the skids. Facing enraged immortals, epic battles against hell's most vile creatures, and the dread of becoming mortal himself, Cupid teams up with an unlikely band of misfit fallen angels in the hopes of saving himself, the Olympic kingdom, and humans the world over. But can such an inept team of losers finally win when it counts?

Funny, rude, and planted smack in modern times, *God Awful Loser* is a new chapter on the ancient gods' bad — and hugely entertaining — choices. May we never follow in their footsteps.

NOW AVAILABLE AT:
WWW.THREEPOINTSPUBLISHING.COM

Cupid's back and at the top of his game.

The always adored – and now restored – God of Love has a new look, a new attitude, and even a steady girlfriend. With his humiliating dethronement and harrowing banishment behind him, Cupid wants nothing more than to settle in to a comfortable immortality.

But someone has dreamed up a different plan.

With a sea god setting the oceans against him, a drama-loving hanger-on refusing to go away, and the king of the gods ordering Cupid to steal the most powerful relic ever made by the most cunning god ever angered, Cupid and his leading lady, Tamara, must join a new cast and crew to face their most challenging mission yet. The stage is set for an epic performance, but just who is writing this script? And will Cupid and his troupe figure it out before they lose their minds – and quite possibly their lives?

God Awful Thief brings new hilarity and an ever-expanding cast of fickle gods to Cupid's misadventures, potential tragedies, and everlasting comedies. *God Awful Thief* is the second act in the *God Awful* Series of Books.

Word of mouth is crucial for any author to succeed. If you enjoyed this book, please tell your friends and leave a review on your favorite website.

We at Three Points Publishing are grateful for your support.

WWW.THREEPOINTSPUBLISHING.COM